The Black Lion

Patricia and Lionel Fanthorpe

DEDICATION

To Brian Jacks, 6 Dan, Champion Superstar
A magnificent sportsman
An incomparable fighter
And a loyal friend

Cover Design by Kevin Kingston Walker
Photography by Chris Howes
Music for 'The Ballad of the Black Lion' by Justin Beynon

Published by Greystoke Mobray Ltd.,
30 Boverton Street,
Roath Park,
Cardiff,
CF2 5ES.
Telephone: (0222) 498368

Made and Printed in Great Britain by
Hunt Barnard Printing Ltd., Aylesbury, Bucks.

ISBN 0 906901 00 6

To Ann and Jim, Best Wishes

The Authors

Patricia Fanthorpe was born in Beetley, Norfolk, in 1938, and married Lionel in 1957. They have two daughters, Stephanie Dawn (1964) and Fiona Mary (1966). Her own favourite writer is Edgar Rice Burroughs. Her first literary ventures were the co-authorship of various textbooks on metrication, office management, and a payroll guide. *The Black Lion* took over seven years to write, and it was Patricia's quiet determination which steered it through those years.

Patricia Fanthorpe.

Lionel Fanthorpe was born in Dereham, Norfolk, in 1935. He sold his first story in 1952 and has since written nearly 200 novels and collections of shorts. He has worked as a dental technician, factory machinist, farmworker and lorry driver. He has also been a journalist, a lecturer for Cambridge University Board of Extra-Mural Studies and an Industrial Training Manager. He trained as a teacher at Keswick College of Education and took an Open University degree. Currently he is Head of a Comprehensive High School in Cardiff. He was one of the invited speakers at *SEACON* (37th World SF Convention) at Brighton in 1979, and Guest of Honour at *TERRACON* in Leeds in the same year. His main hobbies are Power Lifting and Judo at which he has a Brown Belt awarded by Brian Jacks.

Lionel Fanthorpe

Contents

DERL WOTHOR

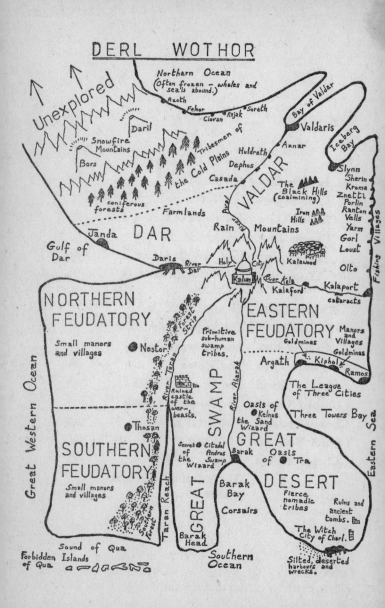

Unexplored

Northern Ocean
(Often frozen — whales and
seals abound.)

Azoth
Felnor Rajak Soreth
Clovan

Bay of Valdar

Valdaris

Iceberg
Bay

Daril

Snowfire
Mountains

Bors

coniferous
forests

Tribesmen of
the Cold Plains

Aznar

Huldreth
Dephos

Casada

VALDAR

The
Black Hills
(coalmining)

Iron
Hills

Slynn
Sherin
Kroma
Znetti
Porlin
Ranton
Vells
Yarm
Gorl
Loust

Olto

Fishing Villages

Farmlands

Janda

DAR

Gulf of
Dar

Daris

River
Dar

Rain

Mountains

Holy

Kalun

City

River Kala

Kalawood

Kalaford

Kalaport

cataracts

NORTHERN
FEUDATORY

Small manors
and villages

Nestor

Forest
Strip

River Taran

Primitive
sub-human
swamp
tribes.

EASTERN
FEUDATORY

Goldmines

Argath

Kiphol

Ramos

Manors
and
Villages
Goldmines

The League
of Three Cities

Great Western Ocean

Thosan

SOUTHERN
FEUDATORY

Small manors
and villages

Ruined
castle
of the wer-
beasts.

Taran Reach

GREAT SWAMP

River Abarak

Secret Citadel
of the of
Swamp Andros
Wizard Swamp
Wizard

Oasis of
Kelnos
the Sand
Wizard

Barak

GREAT

Oasis
of
Tra

Three Towers Bay

Eastern Sea

Barak
Bay

Corsairs

Barak
Head

Southern
Ocean

DESERT

Fierce
nomadic
tribes

Ruins
and
ancient
tombs.

The Witch
City of Charl.

Silted, deserted
harbours and
wrecks.

Sound of Qua

Forbidden Islands
of Qua

Chapter One

The Medallion

An old man was staggering slowly towards my bench. He was enveloped in a thick brown robe topped by a crudely shaped hood. The November wind pulled it back from his face to reveal a grey beard. He had an aesthetic nose and deeply sunken eyes. I wanted him to turn away – I was in no mood for religious eccentrics – but he continued relentlessly towards me and slumped down on to the rain soaked wood. He was exhausted or seriously ill – perhaps both – but he seemed to be trying to say something. It took him several minutes to get his breathing under control, and then a thin, almost transparent hand emerged from the end of his sleeve and touched my arm. Our eyes met, and I experienced a strong sensation of having seen him somewhere before. He reminded me vaguely of the prison chaplain.

'At last . . . at last,' he whispered. I wondered whether his words were meant for me or if he was mumbling a fragment of some private thought. He fumbled in a leather pouch hanging from the robe's girdle and withdrew a glittering object about the size of a pocket watch. 'This is rightfully yours, my son; take and use it quickly.' He thrust it into my hand, and rose with difficulty. I was holding a golden medallion into which was set the bas-relief figure of a black lion, so perfectly carved that it seemed alive. When I looked up the old man was nowhere to be seen – yet the park was almost empty, and it scarcely seemed possible that he could have staggered out of sight so quickly.

The medallion began to vibrate in my hand as I turned it over to examine the other side. A man's profile had been carved on it as finely as the lion had been depicted. The vibration increased in frequency, and my grip on the medallion tightened. *My own face was carved there*. The park grew emptier and more silent while I absorbed every detail of that carving, and the vibration continued growing louder. My heart beats and breathing were taking their time from the rhythm of the medallion. The park was acquiring a strange alien quality: as alien as the prison where I'd wasted the last three years.

The urge to hang the medallion around my neck became an irresistible longing: a desire that began in the soul and reached out to the fingertips – as undeniable as death. I looked for a clasp or join in the chain, but it seemed to have been forged in one continuous band. Taking a few links in either hand I pulled it over my head.

There was a sudden plunging sensation, a leaping into deep waters – a feeling of strangeness, of being engulfed. This was followed by an absence of feeling; time was no longer passing. Light came back first, then colour; sound followed later; everything was chaotic and indistinct. There was a sickening spinning movement: involvement in a huge vortex. Gradually the universe settled down again. Slowly, very slowly, chaos gave way to order, and I felt something solid beneath me.

A road, dusty and primitive, was flanked by scrubby hedges and gaunt trees. Crudely cultivated fields of poor, stony soil lay beyond. I became aware of the hardness of the ground and realised that apart from the medallion I'd lost everything I'd been wearing. I moved slowly off the road and looked at the bleak empty fields. They seemed disconcertingly familiar, yet this primitive landscape was unlike anything I could remember seeing before. Conscious memory denied all knowledge of the place, but something deeper than

8

conscious memory was stirring now. I felt more at home here than I had ever felt anywhere. Perhaps I had never previously seen this land, but I knew I belonged. Wherever I was, this was my world.

There were several sets of footprints on the road, and they looked recent. Keeping to the shadow of the hedges I followed the trail. A few paces from my starting point the footprints showed signs of violent activity. I followed drag marks to a clump of bushes and found two bodies – still warm. The first was a woman of about forty-five and she'd been attractive until somebody had hewn her almost in half. The second had been a warrior. He wore a burnished steel breastplate and thick leather tunic reinforced with metal strips and studs. He lay on his shield now and his sword was still in its sheath. The face was hard and heavily bearded. Dead eyes looked upwards with sightless bewilderment. I rolled him over to unfasten the armour and saw the small jewelled dagger buried to the hilt in his back. At the dead woman's girdle hung an empty sheath. It fitted the little jewelled dagger, a woman's weapon.

I struggled into the dead man's armour and studied the marks on the road with renewed interest. The woman appeared to have leapt from the shadow of the hedge and struck without warning – if those small, deep, sandal prints at a tangent to the rest were hers. But there were other small prints still going in the same direction as the larger ones. Had it been some sort of rescue attempt? The hard, bearded face of the dead warrior had failed to arouse my sympathy, and I began to run along the trail of footprints, pleasantly surprised at the ease with which I bounded over the ground. I ran hard for some ten or fifteen minutes and then, rounding a bend, I saw four men, dressed and armed as I was, leading a chained girl – the image of the dead woman, but less than half her age. They stood spellbound at first, staring as though at a resurrected corpse. I was scarcely ten paces away when the first man reacted. He drew his sword and raised the heavy metal shield with a trained defensive movement.

As far as I could recall I'd never used a sword before; I'd never fenced; I couldn't tell a foil from a sabre. Yet now hand and eye co-ordinated with rhythmic precision. My opponent's shield went spinning away as mine struck the edge of it. The arm that had held it hung numbed and useless. He parried the first stroke automatically, going back awkwardly and trying to ride the blow. It was too hard to be ridden. His helmet split like an eggshell as my blade buried itself deep in the cleft skull. I killed the second man almost casually with the shield edge. The third was holding the chain that secured the girl. I struck before he could release it and severed his arm above the elbow. He looked unbelievingly at the wound. Before understanding could dawn, my sword point flicked forward, emerged behind his neck for an instant and withdrew again like the tongue of a steel snake. The fourth man began to run. He had taken only three paces before I felt intuitively that he must not escape, that he must not live to tell what he had seen. He was taking his fourth and final pace when I hurled the sword into his back and watched it penetrate to within a hand's breadth of the hilt.

The girl meanwhile was calmly removing a key ring from the belt of the man who had held her chain. I took the keys from her and unlocked the manacles securing her wrists. The skin was lacerated and bleeding. I glanced at the handcuffs before flinging them away in disgust. The metal bands were lined with short sharp spikes.

She looked at me searchingly for a moment, then her eyes seemed to light up with recognition mixed with something like a religious fanaticism. She started to cry and fell at my feet: a priestess in the presence of her god.

'Oh, my Lord,' she sobbed, 'you have returned to us. The Lion has come back to his people, and the long darkness shall end.'

'Please stand up.' She knelt for a moment, her face against my knee, black hair cascading over my feet, the warmth and wetness of her tears against my skin. Then she rose and stood in front of me, quiet and full of dignity. 'I do not

10

understand,' I said. 'Why do you say the Lion has returned?'

She looked puzzled.

'My Lord does not understand?'

I told her what I could remember about my trial and the man I had killed fighting in a dockside pub. I told her about my prison years and the grey-green drabness of a cold park bench. I described the old man who had looked like a priest, and I showed her the lion medallion. I told her of my strange leap between the worlds and of finding myself here by the side of the road less than an hour ago. I spoke briefly of the two bodies and following the footprints. When I had finished she no longer looked bewildered, but her strong young face was grave.

'There is much to tell you, my lord, but I need your help desperately while there is still time. Eldon, my father, was one of your loyal officers, a garrison commander. He will die at sunset if we cannot release him.'

'How far?' I asked, looking at the sun where it hung twenty degrees above the horizon.

'We are almost half a day's march from Kalaford.'

'Are there horses here?'

'The League of Three Cities have taken all they could find and there is no time to search.'

'Then we will run.'

I wiped the sword and sheathed it firmly, slung the shield over my back and took the girl's hand.

'I don't even know your name.'

'I am called Amana; it means daughter of the river.'

'I was called Sable, Mark Sable.'

'Here you are called the Black Lion, Lord of Dar and King-Brother of the North.'

We had turned back heading towards the place where I had re-entered my world. Amana ran well. Her young body rippled with lithe feline muscles like an Amazon princess. Her long sun-bronzed legs carried her over the ground with a light, rhythmic grace. She ran like a Maenad on a Greek vase, but with more purpose. There was something of Diana the huntress in her. Her firm full breasts rose and fell as she

11

breathed. Her hair streamed out behind her. At first we talked as we ran and I began re-learning the background of my world. Sometimes, a chord of deep memory stirred as Amana spoke of mountains and ice-locked bays. Some names evoked the warmth of resurrected friendship, others deep, brooding, implacable hatred.

I learned that the whole area was called Derl Wothor and that it was either a large island or a peninsula. Amana spoke of surrounding oceans in all places but the north-west where the Snow Fire Mountains towered thousands of feet above the coniferous forests. The twin volcanic peaks, Bors and Daril, dominated the Snow Fire range; their summits glowed like the aureoles of a passionate earth goddess below coverlets of volcanic smoke. These Snow Fire mountains were riddled with caves where sub-men lived out primitive bestial existences. What lay beyond these mountains no man knew, though Amana believed that there were secret maps in the ancient library at Kalun the Holy City, deep in the heart land of Derl Wothor on the upper slopes of the Rain Mountains. As Amana talked I built up a composite picture of the whole country: whale and seal hunters in tiny villages on the ice-locked northern coast to the east of the Snow Fire mountains; wild nomadic tribesmen governing cold plains immediately to the south of them; the city-ports of Janda, and Daris, my own capital city, built where the wild white torrent of Dar poured into the Western Ocean. A fertile triangle of rich temperate farmlands reached up from the estuary, the deep and ship-filled Gulf of Dar, until its apex joined the wide bend of the River Aval, boundary between the twin kingdoms of Dar and Valdar. She told me of Valdar's industries and ports: its Black Hills of coal and its Brown Hills of iron, its farms and its fishing.

Her voice changed as we spoke of the lands below the Rain Mountains. South of the rivers Dar and Kala lay loyal feudatories, owing allegiance to the King-Brothers of the north, the Golden Tiger of Valdar and the Black Lion of Dar. I interrupted to question her about this, and discovered that the two rulers were traditionally selected *by reincar-*

12

nation. The High Priest of Kalun would find the reborn Lion or Tiger as soon as possible after the previous holder's death. For generations the system seemed to have worked well, one monarch's life span overlapping that of his younger King-Brother and offering protection while the boy grew to manhood. But the dark powers of the far south, waging constant war against the reincarnate kings, had conspired with Andros the Swamp Wizard, Lord of Evil, and devised a means of transmitting the dying Lion's immortal essence between the worlds so that he would be reincarnated in some alien bourne of time and space.

I knew then why the angry fist of a feudal war lord had struck hard enough to kill the man who had crossed him in an argument. I knew now why that same reincarnated warrior-king had established his reputation in jail as the man the barons left alone. I knew too the identity of the old man in the park: the High Priest of Kalun himself who had walked the terrible roads between the worlds to find me and bring me home.

Amana was talking less now as we ran. Her breathing was harder and deeper. There was pain in her eyes as she forced her beautiful young body to the limits of endurance. I realised with a jolt that we must have covered seven or eight miles but I was scarcely conscious of having made any effort. For her the pace must have been murderous. I reckoned that Derl Wothor had a lower gravity than Earth. That would also have accounted for the one-sidedness of my fight with Amana's captors. She had stopped talking altogether now and staggered as she ran. She gulped air desperately, running her heart out. I scooped her up into my arms without slackening the pace and was surprised by her lightness. I guessed her weight at 50 kilogrammes but she felt like a young child in my arms.

'You can go faster without me, Lord,' she panted.

'I can't find the way without you; lie still and breathe.' She felt good in my arms, and there was strong animal attraction in the hot womanly smell from her sweating body. The feel of her arms around my neck was inviting and I

13

smiled down at her as I ran. 'How far now?' She looked at the sun before answering.

'We shall be in time, Lord. My father shall not die.' She started crying again, but it was with hope and happiness this time. 'You will see Kalaford from the top of this slope.'

As we covered the next mile she told me a little of the League of Three Cities, Argath, Kiphol and Ramos: their cruelties, their goldmines and their slaves. She spoke of their vast mercenary armies, their great castles and the fortresses commanding Three Towers Bay.

She told me of the war, and of how the former Black Lion had died in battle over thirty years ago, of how the Golden Tiger had fought on through lonely years to keep the power-hungry south at bay. Now the Tiger was growing old; too many feudal lords were struggling against him and one another for increased independence. The tribesmen of the plains were not willing to ride unless the Lion led the armies of Dar. Only a few garrison commanders clung to the old vision of the Twin Kingdoms. Her father was one of the few. He had held Kalaford since before she was born. The long absence of the Golden Tiger on a punitive expedition across the western swamps of Abarak had tempted the armies of the League into the Eastern Feudatory of Valdar. The garrison at Kalaford had fought grimly but numbers had finally told and the League's vast mercenary, slave and conscript army had seized the ford. Their road to Slynn and Valdaris was open; the kingdom of Valdar itself was in danger.

The League's local Commander, an Argathian noble named Melak, was a devious thinker.

'I was taken to my father's cell and chained for the journey,' said Amana. 'They told him I would be taken to Argath, whipped, branded and sold in the slave market.'

'To work in the gold mines?' I asked.

'To serve in their torture brothels . . . to be burnt alive, or die as a galley slave when I was no longer new enough to amuse the customers . . . ' She shuddered. 'As I was dragged out they told me to watch the sunset. My father was to sink with the sun.'

14

'What's their execution plan?'

'I think they intend to drown the garrison survivors in the ford they defended.'

We reached the top of the long slope and looked down at the River Kala; the small, walled town nestled around the crossing place. I judged that we were now just over a mile away. There was still half an hour before the fatal sunset. I set Amana down and we moved stealthily along the shadows of the hedges until we reached the wall. The gates were still open about fifty yards to our right, but a group of black-armoured Argathians stood by the gate house. I looked at the wall top again: fifteen feet at the most.

'Wait here,' I said softly, 'and guard these.' I took off the steel breastplate and laid the sword and shield beside it. I paced out a short run and sprang at the wall. If anything I had underestimated the effect of the reduced gravity. My hands locked easily over the stone parapet and I pulled myself quickly to the top. Another moment and I had dropped inside the town. This area near the wall appeared to be a dump or waste ground of some sort, and there was no one in sight. Among the rubbish I found two or three short pieces of rope and leather. I knotted them together and went back to the wall. This time I judged the jump better and dropped the improvised rope to Amana. She picked up my sword and armour and held the rope tightly. I hauled her up, and we descended to the waste ground where I refastened the breastplate.

'Where are they holding your father?'

'This way.' She led me through a maze of narrow streets which bore marks of recent savage fighting.

*　　*　　*

'The time is almost up, old man.'

Eldon looked up without fear or regret.

'It is not over yet, Melak.'

'Have you thought of your daughter's progress?'

'I have thought of little else – save the return of my lord, the Black Lion.'

15

'You speak like an old woman who seeks comfort from the spirits of the dead. The soul of the Lion was reborn on a world across the galaxy . . . He will never return to Derl Wothor. Your hope is built on illusions, so let us consider your fears for they are real.'

'Your voice is only a little wave, Melak. It splashes against this old rock without effect.'

'I intend to destroy your mind before disposing of your body, old man. We will talk of this daughter of yours, this Amana. We will picture her adventures. My men will have used her already, of course, to lighten their journey to Argath. She will have been forced to submit to them repeatedly.'

'You still know very little of the women of Kalaford, Melak,' smiled the old warrior. 'Amana has loved men before, and our warriors of the north appeal to women more than your half-men of the south.' The Argathian recoiled and drew in his breath sharply. His eyes narrowed.

'So your young she devil is no stranger to the life that waits for her, but will she welcome the caress of the lash and the kiss of the branding iron so eagerly? We flog and brand every slave brought into the market.'

'We do not welcome pain, but we live with it when we must and conquer it if we can. I love my child, and I would give my life to free her – but I do not fear for her spirit.'

'Then fear for her body, old fool. Hot irons and the lash are only the beginning of long torments which end inevitably with death at the stake, at the oars of our galleys, or in the arena.'

'Melak, you are only a maggot that disturbs the dead, and of less worth than the dust. Don't be deceived because my hair is grey. At the ford I slew a score of your soldiers – and the least of them was stronger than you. Come within reach while life remains and you'll not see me die.'

Melak's face lost some of its colour and he took a hesitant pace back. Then he laughed uneasily and looked through the grating at the setting sun.

'You talk too much, old one. We go to the ford to close

16

your mouth with mud. Guards, fetch out the prisoners.'

There was a crash as I splintered the prison door with a roof beam that had fallen in the fighting. The Argathian guards turned open mouthed to stare at the doorway. I drove at them with the improvised ram and the first two dropped like skittles. A third man was pinned under it as I threw it towards him and drew my sword. A rapturous cry rose from the prisoners as chains rattled against staples and bars. Amana was close behind me; she snatched a dying man's sword as I strode across his body to reach the remaining guards. Confined in the prison's ante-room there was little space for footwork and no refuge to which the Argathians could retreat. They fell like cattle in a slaughterhouse; I killed three; Amana cut down the fourth as she ran to her father's cell.

Eldon was chained securely at wrists and ankles. Melak had drawn his bejewelled ceremonial sword and held the blade against the old warrior's throat from behind.

'Stop,' he shrieked desperately, 'stop or I'll kill him.'

'Don't stay your hand for me, Lord,' called Eldon. 'I'll still live long enough to see you tear out his heart. You have returned and Amana is free – could man know greater joy in death?' His earlier threats to Melak had not been empty words; his shoulders were wide and the knotted muscles of his arms showed through his torn tunic. His manacled wrists came up swiftly, interposing the steel shackles between blade and throat. Then he had Melak's hand between his and there was a scream as small bones splintered. Eldon stooped as far as his chains would allow and heaved the crippled Argathian over his shoulder. Melak landed at my feet; stunned and winded by the fall. Before I could move, Amana stood across him, striking and stabbing, beside herself with fury. Blood welled across the floor but her sword continued to rise and fall.

'Daughter.' There was gruff mock severity in Eldon's voice. 'Daughter, this is no time to carve small meat for young hounds. Release my men and me to greet our King as he deserves.'

I stood keeping a watch on the street as Amana took the keys and began unfastening doors and shackles. Then twelve men lined up to salute me. Eight held up swords; four raised strong right arms.

'My Lord,' said Eldon simply, 'I have held this ford in your name, and in the name of your King-Brother the Golden Tiger, for thirty years. My deepest shame was to lose it last night. My greatest joy will be to see you reclaim it: I pledge my sword forever in your service.'

'And mine,' chorused the eleven garrison survivors.

I cannot describe my feelings as I looked at this first nucleus of my army: pride, warmth, gratitude, affection, a sense of mutual belonging and something more. But we were fourteen including Amana against at least a thousand Argathians, if my estimate of the occupying forces was accurate.

'Eldon, we must head north and raise a new army to clear out these Argathians. Where shall we find the nearest loyal men of Valdar?'

'Teryn, leader of the Forest Rangers in Kalawood, is a true man, but he commands only two or three hundred.'

'Will he come at your bidding?'

'Yes, Lord, if I ride in your name.'

'Then take three men, capture horses and ride to Kalawood. Raise the Rangers and return to Kalaford with all speed. Go now.'

'It shall be done,' Eldon's eyes were shining with excitement as he left.

'Amana, where else are loyal men to be found?'

'At Kalaport, where this river meets the sea.'

'How do you reach it?'

'A swift boat will be there by midnight and back by morning, Lord.'

'Take four men and a fast boat. How many can you bring me?'

'Three hundred for certain, Lord, more if the fishing fleet is in.'

18

'Take care, Amana, for you are already precious to me, but go quickly.'

Amana selected her small force and vanished into the twilight streets. I looked at my remaining soldiers.

'Where else can we hope for help?'

'The miners of the Iron Hills love the Golden Tiger and hate the League of Three, Lord,' said the man nearest to me.

'What is your name, friend?'

'I am Candor, my Lord, and I am a miner's son.'

'Then, Candor, take your comrades here and go to the Iron Hills. Bring back to Kalaford every miner who is willing to fight for the North. Be swift, my soldiers.'

'But, Lord . . . '

'Yes?'

'Lord, you will be alone against a thousand enemies.'

'They will not know that. A man alone against many knows he can strike at all. But many hunters seeking one lion often strike their own men in the darkness.'

Candor smiled. 'May every shining spirit in Kalun guard the Lion, King-Brother of the Tiger.' He led his men out into the gathering gloom.

Chapter Two

The Terror by Night

I left the prison and slid noiselessly along the wall. At that moment I had no clear plan other than to erode the morale of the Argathians and pick them off one or two at a time until my armies arrived in the morning.

I moved down a short street of terraced houses built from natural stone and rough hewn timber. The sturdy oak doors were closed and most windows were shuttered. The street grew darker with each passing minute, and as the darkness deepened I began to feel increasingly excited. At the end of the street stood two Argathian sentries; one looked down towards the ford; the other was covering an arc of about seventy degrees with regular movements of his head. I threw a small stone high enough to land on the building opposite. Both looked up, startled at the sound, and there was a brief whispered discussion. Then the taller of the two went forward alone to investigate. He disappeared into a narrow passageway between the buildings as I crept quietly behind the remaining sentry and clapped a hand over his mouth. He struggled vainly for a second until I brought my other hand up behind his head and jerked hard. There was a click and a stifled grunt. I felt the body go limp and lowered it quietly before salvaging the sword and dagger. Sheathing my original blade, I waited for the other sentry to appear at the mouth of the passage across the street.

'I see nothing,' he called out softly. The sword whistled as it cut the air separating us. There was a loud clang as it struck his breastplate, followed by a cry of pain and surprise. The sentry thudded back against the wall and collapsed into an ungainly sitting position. I flung the dagger at him, and heard another cry of pain before disappearing back into the darkness. Putting my shoulder to the next door I encountered I forced it inwards and stepped over the threshold of one of the small terraced houses.

The interior was almost dark, but a rushlight burned in one of the far corners and silhouetted against it was the figure of an old man. As my eyes adjusted to the gloom, I could just make out a parchment scroll in his fingers, close to the dim light.

He looked around slowly, and stared towards me in surprise.

'You are dressed as a soldier of Argath, but my mind contradicts my sight. Who are you?'

I secured the door with a heavy rustic chair and walked towards the small table that held the light.

'Your tread is as the tread of Dar, and you stand like a war lord, not a soldier of the line. The uniform of Argath does not rest easily upon you.' His voice had risen half an octave and he rose from the table trembling with excitement.

He held the rush light cautiously towards my face, then gasped, lowered it to the table and fell awkwardly to his knees.

'My Lord, you have returned across the galaxies. The High Priest trod between the stars to seek for you, walked through eternity to search for you. Oh, my Lord, I have longed and prayed for this day . . .'

I put a hand on the old man's arm and helped him back into his chair.

'The enemies of Dar are masters of my faithful Kala-ford until sunrise,' I said softly. 'I intend their attack on my garrison to be a mistake the survivors will never forget and never dare to repeat. There shall be a new saying in Argath from tomorrow until the League of Three Cities is destroyed: *Nothing is as terrible as a night in Kalaford.*'

'May the High Gods of Kalun be with the Black Lion,' intoned the old man. 'I will find food and drink for you, my Lord.'

'I'll take a slice of bread and a cup of wine with you, if you have them. I have not eaten since my return.'

The old man shuffled off into a back room and reappeared with a thick slice of wholemeal bread on a wooden platter. In his other hand he held a goblet of wine; it gleamed a wholesome red in the faint light. Both wine and bread tasted home-made. I had not realised how hungry I was until the bread was between my teeth.

'Can you spare another slice, friend?'

'Gladly, master.' He shuffled off into the back room again while I sipped his strong, sweet, red wine. When he returned he also carried a bow and a quiver of black arrows. He held them out to me.

'My Lord, when you were old in your previous life, I was an archer in the Royal Guard of Dar. It is many years since I had strength enough to pull this bow. I see that you have only the armour of Argath. It is fitting that the Black Lion of Dar should fight with the straight black shafts of Dar.'

I finished the bread and wine and received the old man's gift in both hands.

'What is your name, Royal Bowman of Dar?' He stood a little taller in the rushlight. His shadow lengthened on the wall.

'I was Cronan, Captain of the Third Company, Lord.'

'You are still Captain Cronan of the Third Company.' In a sudden time-defying vision I saw him as a young bowman again, proudly wearing the black uniform of Dar in battle after battle, growing old in the service of the King-Brothers of the North. I saw him retiring here to the quiet of Kala-ford, alone with his pension and his memories. I took the parchment he had been reading. It was his Captain's Commission, sealed with the royal seal of Dar, the imprint of a lion in black wax. I pressed my thumb symbolically over the black seal and handed him the parchment.

'You shall eat again on the high seats of the Royal Guards of Dar, Cronan the Faithful.' His eyes were moist as he pulled himself to attention to receive back his commission. From a cupboard he brought out a Darian sword belt. A keen blade rested in the black steel scabbard.

'I have kept it sharp and clean, Lord. Once a soldier of Dar always a soldier of Dar.' I buckled on the sword and tried its weight. It was a vastly superior weapon to the one I had flung at the sentry.

'Thank you, Cronan. I shall borrow it until morning. Secure your doors when I am gone; the town is full of enemies. Tomorrow I shall return your blade and set you on the road to Dar. One day we shall feast there together, and you shall remind me of old battles that I have forgotten.'

I shook his hand and left silently by the back way into a narrow alley. Moving softly I made my way towards a lighted building in the distance. As I approached I heard laughter and raised voices singing. It was mocking laughter and the songs were the cruel songs of Argath, Kiphol and Ramos. There was no humour and no music in the noise. From time to time there were crashing sounds, thuds, curses and cries of fear or pain.

Through the tavern window I saw twenty Argathian soldiers, perhaps more. The landlord, fat, bald and terrified was trying to serve a dozen men at once. A soldier tripped him; his tray went flying; there was a roar of laughter and a flurry of sandals as the Argathians kicked the sprawling figure. A cold-eyed junior officer looked angrily at the beer stain on his tunic. He drew a dagger and struck viciously at the landlord's hand where it rested on a chair seat as he tried to pull himself up. There was a scream of pain. The dagger pinned the hand to the chair. The landlord blinked and stared in disbelief.

'Help me,' he sobbed.

A door behind the bar opened quickly and a girl appeared, dark skinned and beautiful, a nomad from the Great Desert, south of the Oasis of Kelnos, by the look of her. She wore a

23

headband of golden discs, interspersed with small jewels, and an ornate dancing costume – an entertainer. She looked like one of the travelling artistes who move from town to town and from tavern to tavern in the Two Kingdoms.

'Go back, Ambala,' shouted the landlord, but she walked disdainfully through the Argathians and put her hand firmly over his injured one. With a movement that was at the same time quick and gentle, she plucked out the dagger. The landlord slumped to the floor again, semi-conscious. The Argathian officer stepped forward and held out his hand.

'My dagger.'

With a movement too swift for the eye to follow she drew the blade across his palm, cutting almost to the bone. He screamed and clutched the injured hand to his chest. His eyes blazed.

'Get her,' he roared, and Ambala was surrounded by grim-faced Argathian soldiers. She fought like a tigress – as all desert girls can. I knew that every eye in the room was on her as she struck out in all directions with her small hard fists and feet. Her first precise, powerful kick caught the nearest man in the groin and he collapsed gasping on the floor beside the landlord. A crisp punch sent another soldier reeling, his nose broken.

The window was ajar and silently I edged it wider. I fitted the first black arrow to Cronan's bow and drew back the string. No one in the room seemed to hear the faint, musical twang as I fired the arrow. The Argathian nearest the window flung up his arms and crumpled to the floor. The arrow had struck him between the shoulder blades. Its head stood a hand's breadth out from his chest as he slumped. The soldier next to him half-turned towards my window as his companion sank dead to the floor at his feet. My second shaft, fired quickly, went higher than I had intended. Meant for his throat, it tore away teeth and jawbone to lodge at the base of his skull. This time the soldiers near him heard the impact, the strangled gasp of agony and the crash as he fell across the table. Two of them looked directly at me and rushed towards the window with swords drawn.

I had already fitted a third arrow and this took the nearest man straight through one eye. The next hit his companion in the stomach, between the breastplate and tunic belt, just as he struck at me with his sword. His steel grazed my borrowed armour, making a noise like a hacksaw on iron; then the blade slipped from his dying fingers.

Another arrow pinned the Argathian officer dying against the wooden wall on the far side of the tavern. One group of soldiers made for the door, others were crouching behind tables and benches looking for protection from the deadly black shafts. For the time being they had forgottten Ambala and the landlord.

He seemed too bewildered to help himself, but the brown-skinned desert girl thought as well as she fought, her mind as agile as her limbs. Half-dragging and half-carrying him, she retreated through the door at the rear of the counter.

I propped Cronan's bow by the wall and drew both swords, the Argathian blade in my left hand, the strong, true steel of Dar in my right. Seven or eight Argathians had emerged from the tavern door, and their leader was within arm's length when I turned to face him. I feinted with my left, and, as he retreated off balance I brought Cronan's sword round in a terrible whistling arc of death. The sharp, heavy war-steel of Dar, lovingly polished by the old archer severed the Argathian's head like an executioner's axe. It rolled slowly towards the tavern door. The body remained revoltingly upright for a few seconds, blood pumping from the neck.

The Argathians stood frozen with horror waiting for it to fall. In those vital seconds I stabbed left and right at the vulnerable spots between breastplates and belts. Two more Argathians screamed and fell.

The next four came in together in a wild, desperate rush. I threw them back like children with wooden swords. A blade scratched my left hand, but it was scarcely skin deep. I stabbed again with the Argathian blade, then brought the heavy Darian sword round in another fatal arc: grim reaping in a red field. Two men fell at that stroke. The fourth

25

dropped his sword and begged for mercy. I needed a messenger.

'Tell your companions in the tavern that the Black Lion of Dar has returned to reclaim his Kingdom. Tell them that every Argathian I find in Kalaford shall die for invading my realms. Their one hope of life is to return at once to the League of Three Cities, and even there they shall not be safe for long. Go.'

He scrambled to his feet and backed away from me into the tavern. I heard his voice calling hysterically to his companions and then a handful of them stumbled from the tavern, their hands clear of their weapons. They glanced at the bodies of the fallen as they passed and began to run south.

'Tell them,' I roared, 'tell them it is death to be found in Kalaford.'

I retrieved Cronan's bow and strode into the tavern.

There was a swift movement behind me, a volcano erupted at the back of my skull and I dived into an indigo pit. I couldn't have been unconscious for more than a few seconds. As I climbed up out of a confused mist of chair legs and upturned tables, I saw Ambala burying her dagger in one Argathian's stomach while the fat, bald landlord smashed a heavy stone bottle over the head of another.

The throbbing mist receded and I stood up unsteadily. The Argathians I had last seen running south were returning with drawn swords.

'Argathian trickery,' I whispered, a sword in each hand again, and shaking my head to clear it. Ambala's dagger, still red from its last victim, sang past my ear and buried itself in the leading Argathian's throat. The others turned and fled south again; this time it was genuine.

'They had left two men hidden by the door,' explained the landlord. 'One struck you down as you entered.'

'I've been too long away,' I said. 'I'd forgotten the cunning of Argath.'

'My husband killed this one with a wine bottle,' said Ambala proudly. She put her arms around the landlord and looked lovingly into his fat, perspiring face. He was not a very prepossessing specimen, I thought, but I was already impressed by what I'd re-learnt about the women of Derl Wothor.

'I bought her from a slave merchant near Kelnos when I had gone south to buy wine,' said the landlord, as though explaining something. 'She was destined for the torturers of Kiphol.' He put his arm around the girl. 'Who could let anything so lovely fall into their hands?'

'He spent all his wine money to buy me,' she interrupted, 'then when we reached Kalaford, he set me free and said I could stay at his inn until I found work or a husband. Who would not love such a man?'

Suddenly I saw beyond his fat, perspiring face, and slow, ungainly body. Just for a moment my mind reached his; I saw him then as Ambala saw him, and I understood them both. The moment ended, and I was back in the urgent reality of staying alive in Kalaford until morning and inflicting maximum damage on the Argathians at the same time.

Chapter Three

The Battle of Kalaford

It was a night of slaughter and swift, silent movement: an arrow here, a sword-thrust there. Two men on patrol did not walk wide enough at a dark corner. A drowsy sentry on a balcony was caught by the ankles and flung headlong to his death. A watcher by the river was held face down beneath it. Three score men of Argath fell that night by ones and twos to the sinister, shadowy Nemesis that moved around the streets of Kalaford.

As the first grey light of dawn began diluting the darkness which had been my protection, I headed north-west out of the town along a rough track which looked as though it might be the road to Kalawood. Within minutes I heard, or rather felt, the unmistakable vibration of marching feet. They did not march like the feet of a disciplined army. They were purposeful and they hurried, but they did not move in step.

As the light improved I made out a rough column of men, about 200 strong, running and walking down the long, gentle slope towards me.

At the head of the column strode Eldon deep in conversation with a tall, gaunt, craggy-featured man in his forties. He was clad in leather from head to foot. His right arm ended in a steel hook which glinted in the grey light. As I watched I could see Eldon was doing most of the talking. His companion either nodded or answered in gruff mono-syllables. I raised my arm in salutation and called to Eldon. He halted the column silently and ran to greet me. The gaunt man trotted behind him.

'My lord, I present to you Teryn, leader of the Forest Rangers of Kalawood.'

Teryn bowed and raised his hook in salute.

'Welcome back, my Lord. It is good to serve the Black Lion of Dar again. Death to his enemies!'

For Teryn that was a long speech.

'What are your orders, Lord?' asked Eldon. 'Do we wait for the other armies or strike now?'

'We strike now. I have spent the night disturbing the Argathians and few of them have slept – save those who will not wake again. They will be in no mood to meet 200 Rangers.' The light had been improving all the time, and the sun was now a pale yellow secant in the eastern sky. I pointed to the town. 'We will skirt Kalaford to the east and cross the river with the sun behind us. Then we shall attack from the south-east where they least expect to see northern Rangers. Come!'

Our column moved away south-east and headed for the river. Above the steep, grassy banks of the Kala we halted again.

'Eldon, Amana's fishermen from Kalaport will be coming by water?'

'Yes, Lord.'

'Wait for them here. Tell them where we are and give them my orders to attack from the east, by the river gate, where their experience of water will give them most advantage.'

'As you command, Lord.'

'Then find a horse, if you can, and ride north to meet Candor's miners; lead the attack from that side.'

'All shall be done, Lord.'

I watched him walking eastwards along the river bank in the direction of Kalaport to meet Amana's fleet; then I led

Teryn's Rangers across the Kala and westwards towards the town. As I scaled the wall again I found it hard to realise that less than a day had passed since the medallion had brought me back to Derl Wothor and my Kingdom of Dar. Memories of Earth were receding, fading into an unreal, dreamlike limbo.

My night's work had not been wasted. Stories of the killer who struck unexpectedly from the darkness had undoubtedly been enlarged in the telling. The Argathians, unnerved and shaken, were combing the interior of the town for me, looking for a secret enemy in their midst. They had neglected to guard their southern walls. Surely their enemies, unled and unorganised, lay to the north? Nothing lay to the south but frightened peasants in the Eastern Feudatories, unprotected by Lion or Tiger and open to the territorial ambitions of the League of Three.

There was a small gate fifty metres away to my left as I crouched on the wall. I called instructions over my shoulder to Teryn and dropped lightly to the ground. Three men guarded that gate. Three black arrows from Cronan's bow and the gate was clear. I slid back the bolts and turned the wooden spar. The gate opened quietly, and Teryn's Rangers were in Kalaford.

'Straight across to the River Gate,' I ordered. 'We need a bridgehead to the seaward side of the ford so Amana's men can land.'

The first real resistance we encountered was an Argathian patrol of about twenty men in a narrow street running northeast. Half stayed to fight; the others raced away to raise the alarm. Their voices were shrill as we heard them screaming, 'Rangers of Kalawood! Rangers in the town!'

Teryn fought like a man who had no real interest in whether he lived or died. He had unscrewed the hook he normally wore and replaced it with a double-headed battle axe on a steel shank about half a metre long. He stood unconcerned and imperturbable in the centre of the Argathians, cutting at them as methodically as if he were felling trees. Swords and spear points glittered around him but he paid

30

them no attention. Again and again the axe fell, and an Argathian fell at every stroke.

I killed only two of the ten: Teryn and his Rangers destroyed the rest. We reached the end of the narrow street, but at the crossroads Argathians attacked us in force from three different directions. Slowly but surely we cut our way through them, moving always north-east towards the river gate.

Eventually an accurate estimate of the size of our force must have got through to the Argathian commander – whoever he was – who had replaced Melak. The southerners were attacking us on all sides and some thirty or forty Rangers were already dead or too seriously wounded to fight.

'If the fishermen aren't at the river gate within the hour,' panted Teryn, 'we may have to cut right through and wait for them outside the town.'

'We've already taken all the Argathians can throw at us, and we're still advancing.'

'Yes, Lord.' He fell silent and worked away doggedly with his axe. Step by step we moved towards our objective.

'Lord, I see the River Gate ahead.' It was a bright-eyed young Ranger on my right who had shouted.

'Forward!' I felt like a tired horse that has seen his stable across the pastures. The blade I'd borrowed from Cronan turned in my hand like a living thing, and more Argathians fell before it. The way opened a little.

'Forward!' The houses were thinner here by the river. There were open spaces where the Kalafordians had strolled in happier times.

Teryn and I formed the Rangers into a flying wedge. My sword and his axe were its cutting edge. The Argathians fell back yet again. The Rangers pressed exuberantly forward. We had reached the River Gate.

There was a lull for five or ten minutes, and then the Argathians rallied. A hail of spears and arrows sent Teryn's Rangers diving for cover beneath the arches of the bridge from which the River Gate hung. The Rangers unslung their bows and sent off a deadly rain of arrows in return, but the

Argathians had vastly superior fire power and our arrows were few. They could not be wasted merely keeping Argathian heads down. The enemy were moving their marksmen to better positions, and Rangers were falling steadily as their cover no longer protected them from new angles of attack. Three Argathian bowmen in particular were causing havoc among our foresters. These three were high on a watchtower, south of the River Gate, and protected by tall battlements. Even the black shafts Cronan had given me would not dislodge them.

'Come with me, and guard my back, Teryn. Rangers, give us covering fire.'

'Where, Lord?'

'The Watchtower.'

An avalanche of Rangers' arrows stopped the Argathian fire for precious moments as I sprinted for the tower door. Teryn, lean and gaunt, ran like the wind. It was his axe that smashed the tower door while my sword felled the two sentries beside it. I was first as we scrambled up the stairs. The high landing was guarded, but I hurled the Argathian soldier to his death at the foot of the tower. Behind me I heard Teryn's axe clashing against the swords of our pursuers on the stairway. One of the three bowmen turned to the upper doorway and released a shaft at point blank range. It grazed my shoulder as my sword split his helmet. Without changing direction of the stroke, I caught the second archer with a blow from the knurled steel counter-weight on the base of the hilt. A kick that would have cracked a millwheel took the third man in the groin; he collapsed in slow motion, clawing the air in soundless agony. Teryn reached the doorway, and I heard the last of his immediate pursuers thudding down the stairs. Angry voices sounded from the stairwell, but no one came after us. Teryn emptied the Argathian quivers beside me, before heaving the inert bowmen over the parapet.

The tower was an ideal vantage point, although the short, light arrows of Argath were less effective than the black shafts of Dar. I picked off more Argathians with Cronan's bow. Over the sounds of the battle below us I heard Teryn's voice.

'Why no pursuit yet?' he grunted, half to himself.

Before I could answer, I smelt smoke and saw it curling up the stairs.

'They've fired the tower, Lord,' announced Teryn grimly.

*   *   *

Amana, Daughter of the River, was travel-stained and exhausted, her raven hair soaked, dishevelled, and streaked with mud and dirt. The short tunic she wore had originally been white; it was indelibly marked now with sweat, blood-stains and river water. She was cut, bruised and grazed in a score of places, and her feet were bleeding where she had lost her sandals among dense undergrowth in the darkness. It had been a desperate thirty miles from Kalaford to the coast.

She had lost her boat and her escort trying to negotiate the short vicious cataract ten miles downstream from Kala-ford. Normally the small boats plying their trade on the Kala were lifted clear of the cataract and carried along the bank for a few yards. Amana's party had misjudged their position in the darkness, and the cataract had been upon them before they realised what was happening. In the swirl-ing darkness they had capsized. Amana, powerful swimmer that she was, had struggled ashore, but of her escort there was neither sight nor sound. She had weighed the chance of saving them against the importance of reaching Kalaport and bringing the fishermen's militia swiftly to Kalaford. Reluctantly, she had abandoned the missing soldiers and set out for Kalaport on foot. Willpower and courage had carried her twenty miles to the coast, hugging the river bank most of the way in case she lost her direction.

She stood now in the darkness beside the town gates and knocked desperately on the heavy iron-studded wood.

'Who seeks admission at this hour?'

The gate-keeper's voice was suspicious.

'Amana, daughter of Eldon of Kalaford. I bring a message

3   33

from the Black Lion of Dar.' She was gasping for breath between every word. A torch appeared through a watchman's hole in the wall beside the gate.

'You are alone, girl?'

'Quite alone. I lost my boat at the cataract, and my companions were drowned. I have come the rest of the way on foot. Hurry, for the sake of the Gods of Kalun. We need your militia at Kalaford. Argath has overrun the garrison.' She was gasping for breath again. 'Please let me in.' The torch was withdrawn and she heard running feet on stone stairs. The gate opened just enough to admit her and slammed shut the instant she was through. The bolts and bars were replaced.

'Wife!' shouted the gate-keeper, through the door of the lodge. 'Here's a Kalafordian girl, hurt and exhausted. Tend her while I fetch Bel.'

'Who's Bel?' whispered Amana. She was reeling against the wall. Only now that she had reached her objective was she allowing her body to experience its own exhaustion.

'Captain of the fishing fleet and Captain of the Kalaport Militia,' answered the gate-keeper, disappearing into the night.

A plump, grey, motherly-looking woman stumbled sleepily to the door of the lodge, rubbing her eyes. As wakefulness returned her eyes lost their sleepy look. Her expression became tender and concerned.

'Come in, child, come in. Whatever's happened to you?'

As the gate-keeper's wife heated soup, broke bread, bathed wounds and cut bandages, Amana told her story. Her breathing was under control again by the time she had finished eating. As Amana talked she was gently washed and bandaged, her hair was brushed and braided, and the gate-keeper's wife found her a clean tunic. By the time Bel arrived Amana felt human again. He was a much younger man than she had expected, younger than the Black Lion and far smaller. Quick brown eyes regarded her sympathetically.

'I hope a good welcome makes up for a bad journey,' he

34

said. Suddenly and impulsively Amana hugged the gate-keeper's wife, and kissed her gently on the cheek.

'Thank you,' she said simply. The older woman smiled understandingly.

'What help do you need at Kalaford?' asked Bel.

'As many fighting men as you can send, as quickly as possible. The Black Lion has returned to Derl Wothor.'

'I told you, Bel,' broke in the gate-keeper excitedly, 'she did say the Lion was home again.'

'All praise to the Bright Spirits of Kalun,' exclaimed Bel. 'In the Lion's name every man in Kalaport shall sail with us. Fazor, help me rouse the militia. Praise the Gods the fleet is in! We can raise half a thousand within the hour.' He turned to Amana. 'Rest here until we are ready. My boats will not leave without you. Tell me the rest of your news as we sail.'

Bel and Fazor, the gatekeeper, ran out into the dark streets, waving a torch and ringing the clamorous, brazen handbell that traditionally summoned their militia. 'To arms, Militiamen of Kalaport, to arms!' called Bel as he ran. Amana and the gate-keeper's wife stood in the doorway of the lodge and watched the torchlight until it vanished around a distant corner.

It was still more than three hours before dawn when Bel and Fazor returned to the lodge. Amana stopped only to thank the gate-keeper's wife once more then ran with Bel to the jetty. In the light of a hundred torches she could see scores of small, sturdy fishing boats, each manned by five or six men. Bel helped her into his own vessel, *The Silver Spray*, and gave the sailing order to his fleet. A strong wind from the sea, which Amana had cursed while she had been struggling east against it, now gave the fishing boats a fair turn of speed. They were making seven or eight knots even against the Kala's current. With *The Silver Spray* at their head, 500 loyal Militiamen sailed in support of the Black Lion.

In the pool below the cataract they found the bodies of Amana's escort, and laid the wet corpses on the river bank

35

for burial after the battle. With tears blurring her vision Amana looked searchingly at the dead faces in the flickering torch light. Bel's hand touched her arm gently.

'You could not have done otherwise. If you had drowned searching for them, who would have run through the night to Kalaport? Soldiers of the Lion fight for him in different ways. These men have died for him. You and I live for him. Tomorrow it may be our turn to die. Years pass. Soldiers pass. Battles pass. But the war goes on.' She nodded silently and helped Bel and his men to carry *The Silver Spray* around the cataract.

Dawn came and Kalaford was in sight. The sun rose slowly behind them, and, clear in its long slanting rays, Amana recognised her father running along the river bank to meet them. Bel steered towards the old warrior and Eldon leapt heavily aboard. He and Bel already knew each other.

'Well met, fisherman,' cried Eldon. 'Teryn's Rangers and the Lion have attacked from the south. Your orders are to storm the River Gate. If the Gods of Kalun have blessed the Rangers, they may have cut their way through by now and established a bridgehead for you by the tow path. If not, fight your way ashore and cut south to relieve the Rangers.'

'Aren't you coming with us?' asked Bel.

'I'm going north to meet Danel's miners. Young Candor was sent to fetch them, but it's farther to the Iron Hills than to Kalaport. If all has gone well for him, I'll lead their assault on the north gate.'

'We'll save the last two Argathians for you and Danel,' said Bel.

'Keep safe, girl-warrior; take good care of my Lord the Black Lion, until I return.' He kissed Amana and leapt back to the bank, scrambling awkwardly before regaining his balance on the long, wet grass.

'Your father fights better than he jumps,' laughed Bel, heading *The Silver Spray* out into mid-stream again.

Amana's eyes were straining ahead, trying to make out details of the battle.

'Smoke,' she said ominously.

'And flames,' agreed Bel. His long sea-vision was keen. 'There's a watchtower ablaze by the River Gate.'

With Rangers doggedly holding the river banks, Bel's Militia landed without much difficulty, and began advancing northwards in a broad arrow-head formation, planning to meet up with Danel's miners from the Iron Hills. The Argathians fell back stubbornly and began regrouping to the south of the Kala, just below the ancient ford which had given the town its name. Through the smoke billowing around the blazing tower Amana suddenly recognised the trapped archer ...

*   *   *

'How long, Teryn?'

'Some stones are cracking, Lord. I'll check the stairs.' He disappeared for a moment, then leapt back singed and covered with smoke.

'The centre is a mass of flames, like a furnace. There is no escape down there.'

The Argathians had withdrawn far enough for Amana to reach the foot of the tower, with Bel and the crew of *The Silver Spray*. He shouted orders to his men and they ran to the boats. Amana was back first, a long, thin rope coiled over her shoulders. Ignoring the blistering heat of the smoking stone she began climbing the tower.

'Go back,' I roared, but she climbed like a cat. Gusts of burning air from the narrow windows in the tower singed her black braids as she passed, but she clung to the hot stone like an eagle. She had almost reached us, and I could hear the sobs of pain as she sought for fresh holds with heat blistered fingers and toes.

'Teryn, reach down to her.' I locked my feet under a thick iron stanchion connecting two battlements and gripped Teryn's ankles. Without hesitation the tall Ranger leaned out and hung head downwards. I reached over as far as the iron belay would allow. Teryn's blood-stained axe touched Amana's outstretched fingertips. She clutched it tightly in

37

both hands and kicked her agonised feet away from the hot stones. I pulled Teryn back slowly as though he were a thick living rope going through my hands. As I reached his waist his own strong feet hooked between the battlements, and the long wiry muscles of his legs helped pull Amana up beside us. There was no time to tell her all that I felt about her at that moment, the flames were too close. But I saw Teryn bend his head, and saw his lips touch her hand very gently as he took the rope. He secured it with a forester's knot and began to descend, with the rope twisted around the steel shank of his axe like a friction brake.

'You can't hold a rope with those hands, Amana.'

She shook her head.

'Come on.' She locked her arms around my neck as I stepped out over the parapet and began to abseil down. Two or three stray Argathian arrows passed uncomfortably close to us and ricocheted off the cracking stones.

'Lord, the rope is burning above us,' she cried suddenly. I glanced up instinctively. It was well alight, close to a window slit where flames were spurting. We were only half-way down and I quickened the speed of our descent. The rope burned through and the last few fibres snapped loudly. We clung to each other tightly and waited for the inevitable crash. I tried to stay underneath her to cushion the shock, but when it came it was not an impact at all . . .

'Biggest fish I've ever caught,' said Bel delightedly. He was one of a dozen sturdy fishermen holding a strong net.

As I untangled Amana from the mesh, we heard triumphant shouting from the north. A tall bearded fisherman ran towards us, excitedly shouting, and waving his arms.

'Eldon's here with Danel and hundreds of miners. They've burst the north gate. Argath's in full retreat. The town is ours, Lord.'

Chapter Four

Restoration

Kalaford was busy again after the battle. Citizens were emerging from barricaded cellars and strongrooms; refugees were returning from the rough sanctuaries of Kalawood and the scattered cottages beyond. Friends and relatives feared dead were joyfully reunited. Friends and relatives sought for among the survivors were found among the slain and laid sadly to rest in the heart-shaped cemetery by the banks of the Kala, their heads towards the sacred city of Kalun, prostrate in a last long prayer to the Shining Gods.

I went with Amana and my captains to the house of Cronan, Royal Bowman of Dar. He was looking twenty years younger than when I had first seen him. His old eyes shone with victory. Gravely I handed him his bow and sword.

'I have depended upon this trusty wood and steel through a long battle, and they have served me well. You are like a father to me Cronan, for you fed me and gave me wine; you offered your bow and sword when I had most need. The bow needs oiling now and the sword must be sharpened again.'

The old man took the weapons back with awe and reverence.

'I have always served the King-Brothers of the North,' he said simply.

'When you are ready to travel to my Court at Dar, here is your Royal Warrant of passage.' I wrote out the parchment and signed it on his table. Every coachman in the north would honour it. 'Come when you will and stay as long as you can. Eat at my table. Sing with my troubadours, and sleep beneath my roof.'

'I shall come, Lord, and I shall sing of how the Lion freed Kalaford.' We took our leave of him and went back into the town centre.

Eldon organised the Argathian prisoners into lines in the town square, while I stood on a small outcrop of stone and studied them. Now that the fighting was over I felt no anger towards them.

'Soldiers of Argath, you did wrong to attack my land. You killed and wounded my people. You destroyed much of this, my town. But you, too, have suffered. Many of your companions are dead. Some have already fled south to Argath. This is my judgement. Your wounded will be sent home, and for every five who are injured one fit man shall also be freed to tend them on their journey. The rest of you will stay here as slaves until the damage done to my town has been made good. You will work under the direction of my architects and stonemasons until the Council of Kalaford is satisfied that all is repaired and rebuilt. When that is done, you will be freed and sent back to Argath. The duration of your slavery will depend upon your own efforts. At the worst it should not take longer than a year.' I jumped down from the platform. 'See to it, Eldon, for I have pressing business in Kalun.'

'All shall be done as you command, Lord.'

'There is one more thing. We must improve our communications. Order a line of signal fires to be built and manned along the river to Kalaport and other lines to the Forest and the Iron Hills. When Kalaford is threatened the signal beacons shall be lit, and when the beacons are lit Rangers, fishermen and miners will rally and come swiftly to our aid.'

'It is good, Lord. It shall be done.'

'And now, Eldon, I ride to Kalun, and from there to my own city of Daris. Memories of the long past are beginning to stir deep within my mind. They trouble me, and I am eager to see my home again.' I turned to the woodsman, 'Teryn, Captain of the Rangers.'

'Yes, Lord.' He saluted with the hook which had now replaced his battle-axe.

'Will you ride with me to Kalun, and bring four good Rangers to escort us?'

'At your bidding, Lord.'

'Then meet me at the north gate as soon as you are saddled and ready.' He hurried away to find men and horses and provisions for the journey.

In a shady gateway at the side of the square Amana waited quietly with two horses: a tall black stallion and a chestnut mare. I walked towards her, and she led the horses out to meet me. I noticed that her hands and feet were heavily bandaged and dressed with healing herbs and balsam. She smiled and handed me the stallion's reins.

'May I ride with you, Lord?' I lifted her to the saddle of the chestnut.

'To the ends of the world and beyond.'

Her smile grew radiant, lighting her face like the sun.

'So long a journey may take a life-time, Lord,' she said softly, 'many life-times . . . '

'So be it.' I sprang to the saddle and dug my heels into the horse's sides. She turned the chestnut and followed. We rode together to the North Gate, which bore vivid marks of battle where Danel's men had smashed through.

Teryn and four burly Rangers waited.

'These are the best I have, Lord,' he said simply, 'and we are yours to command.'

'Find me the shortest road to Kalun.'

Two Rangers scouted ahead, and Teryn rode on Amana's left, beside us. The other Rangers brought up the rear.

Eldon had found a sword and longbow for me in the armoury, after I had returned old Cronan's weapons to him. They were of Darian workmanship and almost indistinguishable from those which I had borrowed from the veteran archer.

'Our safest and surest route will lie through Kalawood, Lord,' said Teryn. 'My Rangers know every tree, and for over thirty miles the forest will give us good cover. We ride north first, then due east. When the trees end there is a short range of stony foothills to cross before we reach the Rain Mountains. They lead up to the Holy City itself.'

We reached the wood just before mid-day; the Rangers made a cooking fire and prepared venison. We ate savoury meat and herbs together and rested a few moments under the broad green leaves of the deciduous forest. It was almost as though Teryn could read my thoughts as we looked up together at the green boughs.

'This is a warmer forest than your cold pines of Dar, my Lord.'

'Warmer and kinder, Teryn, and more delicately coloured; yet my dark conifers of Dar hold off the snow and ice with a stark strength that has its own lonely beauty. The tall pines stand like sentinels to guard us against the Snow Fire Mountains and the things that live beneath them.' Memory was returning: this life? Another life? 'Have you ever fought the half-men who come from the caves below Daril and Bors?'

'No, Lord, but my father told me of them when I was a child.' He looked troubled. I laughed and rested a hand on the shoulder above his steel hook.

'A man who cuts down Argathians like wheat, will cut down the beast men of Bors like barley.' We rose, extinguished the fire and resumed our journey.

It was pleasant to ride with Teryn and Amana below the green traceries of Kalawood. The sun reached its zenith and sank slowly towards the western horizon. Its slanting rays silhouetted the peaks of the Rain Mountains and threw golden javelins towards us along their deep-floored valleys.

'It is said that the Shining Spirits of Kalun paint the sunset above the Holy City,' murmured Amana, pointing westwards with a bandaged hand.

42

The view was breathtaking as the sun sank lower over those shining mountains until at last its upper edge was eclipsed by the tallest peaks. Soft, warm, coral pink light spread and suffused the western sky. Long brown shadows glided over the foothills ahead of us.

'We have reached the edge of the forest, Lord,' warned Teryn, 'and, although it is dusk there may be enemies here.'

'What enemies?' I asked.

'Since you were taken from us, Lord, the dark servants of Kelnos and Andros have never left these mountains. It is said they search for some great treasure, known only to priests and wizards, a treasure that was lost when you were taken.'

'We know these things only as legends, Lord. If Zotala, the High Priest, yet lives after his walk between the worlds to find you, he will tell you all,' added Amana.

The last of the trees lay behind us now, and our four Rangers had fanned out ahead in a wide scouting formation. The shadows lengthened as we mounted the lower slopes of the foothills, and walked our horses carefully over the uneven terrain.

'It will be best to make camp, Lord, and start our climb at first light. The horses will not be able to go much higher. I'll send Rostor back with them in the morning.'

We halted in a good defensive position, a narrow 'V' shaped defile which ran back into a cave. I took a firebrand and explored the cave, satisfying myself that it ran back only a few feet into the limestone and had no other entrance. I took first watch with Amana and we sat side by side watching the entrance to the defile. Occasionally, eyes would gleam red and green in the darkness beyond our miniature valley, and we heard low growls and the soft padding of clawed feet.

'They are only mountain wild cats, Lord,' explained Amana. 'They are no danger to a waking man with a good sword.' Despite her reassurances I watched the comings and goings of the eyes carefully. There was an oddly intelligent pattern to them. Were they more than random predators of the night? What strange beings had the dark wizards, Kelnos and Andros, created? What lost treasure did they search for here, among the bleak foothills of the Rain Mountains?

Teryn and Rostor relieved us for the second watch. Only now that we were no longer on duty did Amana and I roll into each other's arms and love with the tender-violence of those who have been too long apart. She was warmth and hunger: vibrant, exciting, innocent and experienced at the same time – a hundred feminine paradoxes resolving themselves simultaneously in the everlasting mystery. The night lasted two heartbeats and two million years.

'Lord, it is dawn.' She wriggled gently out of my arms and pulled on her tunic. I dressed slowly, buckled on my sword and roused Teryn and Rostor. There was more venison stewing with herbs in a pot over the fire. We ate quickly, lined up the horses and watched Rostor set out with them towards Kalawood. Then we began to climb.

Chapter Five

Iban and the Jalnar

The mountains were rough and craggy. Vegetation grew in nooks and crevices, but it became scarcer as we climbed higher. Tough little mountain shrubs and trees miniaturised by the lack of soil clung tenaciously to the gritty slopes. Colour grew rarer as the vegetation thinned out.

A great grey-black carrion bird, vaguely reminiscent of a terrestrial vulture circled ominously above us.

'What's that?' I asked Amana.

'A sandhawk of the Great Desert, Lord.' She frowned.

'You mean it's too far north?'

'Yes, Lord.'

'No ordinary sandhawk, then?'

'Zotala would know for certain, Lord, but I think it may be one of the strange servants of Kelnos the Sand Wizard.'

'Sent to watch us?'

'Not us in particular, but sent to guard the slopes of the Rain Mountains and carry word to Kelnos if any travellers climb these rocks.'

'Dead sandhawks carry no messages.' I aimed carefully and pulled back the powerful Darian bow as far as it would go. The black shaft impaled the great body and brought it crashing to the rocks below. There was a terrible high-pitched scream as it fell; it was more like the cry of a hare in a trap than the sound of any bird. Amana's eyes opened wide at the noise.

'No sandhawk ever called like that, Lord.'

'I agree.' Teryn's keen eyes were directed to the spot where the bird had crashed.

'What do you think?' I asked him.

'Devilry of Kelnos, Lord, one of the wizard's dark watchers ... better dead, and best dead before he saw us.'

'Would the body reveal anything?'

'Nothing worth the time taken to retrieve it, Lord. Our best plan is to reach the Temple of Kalun as quickly as possible. When Zotala speaks with the Lion, the Realm of the King-Brothers shall be more secure than it is now.'

We climbed on through mist that slowly turned to rain. Our world became a world of steep, slippery stone, and I kept close enough to Amana to catch her if she fell, for her bandaged hands and feet were a significant handicap, although she climbed superbly.

'May we eat soon, Lord, I'm hungry?' The rain had soaked her to the skin. The wet tunic clung to her magnificent body; her long black hair gleamed like newly-washed coal; her eyes flashed and sparkled like gemstones; her lips were slightly parted in the warm ready smile that was so characteristic of her. A man of stone could have fallen in love with Amana and stepped out of his quarry into the world of flesh and blood because of her. The rain grew harder, and a rising wind from the Eastern Ocean blew over Kalawood rich with the scent of sea and forest. I held Amana tightly to me on the wet rocks and kissed her.

'Yes, my love, we will rest and eat soon. Look for a dry cave as you climb. I do not relish rain with my meat.'

A few metres more and we found the tall, narrow mouth of a deep cave in the limestone. I went in as far as the light showed, but the cave itself was much more than a surface opening. Without a torch it was impossible to guess how far back into the mountain it penetrated. I wished there had been time to explore it fully, but I had probed far enough to know that we would not be attacked suddenly by some strange denizen of the rock hiding near the cave mouth. If anything lurked deep within the mountain the keen ears of the Rangers would give ample warning of its approach, and I was confident that six swords would be more than a match for it.

There were dry leaves and twigs in the cave and the Rangers were never without the means of making fire. Herbs and meat were soon boiling purposefully together just beyond the reach of the driving rain. Perhaps it was the crackling of the fire or the noise from the miniature cauldron that drowned the suspicious crawling sound from the Rangers' ears, but it was Amana who heard it first. Her eyes opened very wide, and her beautiful body tensed suddenly, like the body of a young lioness that scents food for her cubs. Her lips scarcely parted as she whispered, 'Lord, something moves in the cave.'

I beckoned Teryn and the three Rangers. Swords drawn, we formed a half-circle and waited. Something heavy was slithering along the dark rock towards us ...

We saw its eyes first in the light from the small cooking fire. They were red, flecked with a bilious yellow-green, and they were huge. The body was almost as wide as the cave, leathery, pale and mottled covered with warts and blemishes. The head was hideous and misshapen. The mouth was flabby, loose-lipped and slack, revealing rows of discoloured fangs.

There was something totally *wrong* about the enormous creature, as if it were the product of a diseased mind rather than the result of an evolutionary process.

'Jalnar.' It was Teryn who spoke.

'Made by Andros or Kelnos, Lord,' said Amana, 'made to block the route to Kalun, to prey on the unwary or the exhausted.'

'It'll find us hard to digest, Lord,' said Iban, the youngest of the Rangers whom Teryn had chosen for the journey. He was immensely broad and strong, where most of the Rangers were lean and wiry. I guessed that he was originally of

47

mining stock from the Iron Hills, and had moved south to Kalawood.

'Have you seen Jalnars before?' I asked him.

'Once or twice, Lord. They are dangerous brutes, but we can match them. This one will kill no more lonely pilgrims seeking the Holy One of Kalun.' There was some deep significance in his words. His square jaw set grimly. His eyes blazed. My mind was full of questions, but there was no time – the Jalnar was reaching for us with long, leathery tentacles that originated just below the deceptively slack mouth.

The tentacles snaked out in all directions. I felt one around my leg, like the tendril of a jungle vine. Another groped for Amana. My sword swung and both tentacles were severed. They lay writhing on the floor, oozing a black, viscous fluid. The Jalnar screamed horribly, and its eyes flashed like laser beams.

'Blind it first,' said Iban ruthlessly. He stepped past me and drove his sword powerfully and unerringly deep into the Jalnar's left eye. The malevolent red and green light went out. The blemished monstrosity screamed louder and more balefully than before. Its tentacles became a writhing mass of wildly agitated curling leather, reaching for all of us. The teeth ground in fury. Foul-smelling saliva dripped between the discoloured fangs. The surviving eye glared furiously. Iban was wrapped in half a dozen tentacles. His sword arm pinned by his side. The great muscles of his chest and shoulders strained until his left arm was free. He drew his dagger and began cutting furiously at the tentacles holding his sword arm. The razor edged hunting knife devoured the leather and the Jalnar screamed again, a note tinged with fear.

It had come for food, come to envelop and devour a lonely, exhausted, unarmed pligrim or scholar on his way to the Holy Places. It had encountered the most dangerous fighting machine in Derl Wothor and five of his best warriors.

Iban was leading the attack, but Iban was by no means alone. Even as I watched and admired his efforts, I, too, was cutting hard into tentacles and blemished flesh. The Jalnar's hide was thick but not impenetrable to a keen blade in a strong hand. My blows went in up to the hilt; Amana, knowing hers would not penetrate, struck instead at the narrow stab wounds I had already made. Her blade hacked savagely at the edges of the wounds I had already inflicted: turning stabs into deep, lethal gashes, from which black blood welled out, weakening the Jalnar. Teryn was stabbing with his sword and ripping with his hook. The other Rangers attacked furiously, but still it was Iban who led the slaughter. He fought like a man possessed. His sword arm was free again now and he made a stroke at the surviving eye which would have felled an oak tree. The eye was extinguished, and there was the knowledge of death in the Jalnar's screaming. Iban stood within a metre of the gnashing teeth and hacked resolutely at the skull. Teryn paused for an instant and passed his terrible double headed axe to the young Ranger. The jaws closed around Iban's leg but he paid no heed to the terrible teeth, the axe was already swinging. The blow had begun in the great muscles of his thighs, rippled up through the dynamic strength of his hips and abdomen, and erupted volcanically along arms and shoulders. The Jalnar's skull was six inches thick, but Iban's blow split it like a dry log in a woodyard. He pulled his leg clear of the dead jaw and wiped the axe.

'Thank you, Teryn.'

'I didn't have time to screw it on,' said Teryn, 'and I knew you'd use it well.' He looked admiringly at the cloven skull. 'A good blow, lad, your father would have been proud of you.' I suddenly noticed tears in Iban's eyes. Teryn's hand lay on his shoulder for a moment. 'You would have overcome the beast alone, Iban. Only you or the Lion himself could kill a Jalnar single-handed.'

'A magnificent fight, Iban,' I said softly.

'Thank you, Lord.' His eyes were still wet, and he walked slowly to the cave mouth alone. The rain was falling heavily now and we went out to wash off the foul black blood and ooze from the tentacles, before taking our interrupted meal.

4

Amana stood beside Teryn. Her flashing eyes softened in sympathetic understanding.

'What ails young Iban? What grief does he bear?'

Teryn looked down at her gently.

'You are a good woman, Amana.' He sighed. 'Iban's father was a miner who felt the call to be a priest of Kalun. He forsook his mine and his home and set out on the journey to the Rain Mountains. He took no sword and no dagger, for he wished to be a Priest of Peace. As he rested, a Jalnar killed him. Eventually a wandering priest brought home his tunic and his pack, and told how they had been found. He also said that the High Priest of Kalun had absolved his priests from their vows of pacifism. They still avoid harming their fellow men, if they can, but against the evils of Kelnos and Andros they now wage unremitting war. Iban and his father had quarrelled when his father left home. Iban always felt that he should have gone, too, and seen him safely to Kalun. Iban has been a hunter of Jalnars ever since. He is a modest man. He said he had seen Jalnars once or twice; he has killed a dozen. He goes often from Kalawood to the Rain Mountains to seek them out and destroy them, to make the way safer for pilgrims. I chose him because he knows the mountains well, and no other man, save the Lion himself, could destroy a Jalnar.'

As Teryn finished speaking, the young Ranger returned. The rain had washed his face and no signs of his tears remained.

'We were too hard to digest, Lord,' he said grimly, 'and now there is one accursed Jalnar less.'

'I need men like you, Iban, to keep my mountains safe,' I said warmly.

'Thank you, Lord.' His eyes shone, but this time it was with happiness. 'I am always at your service, Lord.'

We finished eating and climbed on until dusk; the setting sun between the mountains to the west of us lit up the spires and domes of the Holy Citadel of Kalun, another day's journey ahead by the look of it. I held Amana tightly and we looked out together at the sunset and the Holy City from whence the High Priest had walked between the worlds to bring me back.

'Amana.'

'Yes, Lord.'

'Zotala walked the impossible path to restore my Kingdom, but I am grateful to him most because you are part of my Kingdom.' Then she was in my arms again, and I knew that not even the high magic of Kalun was greater than the magic of her love.

Chapter Six

Zotala – High Priest of Kalun

Another day of steady effort brought us to the summit of the curving ridge we had been climbing since leaving Kalawood. Ahead of us in the setting sun the gold-edged silhouette of the Holy City dominated a high, lonely peak in the centre of a vast, rock-strewn crater. The Rain Mountains themselves surrounded the timeless city like a circle of guards or worshippers.

'There is a door in the stone, Lord. It leads to a flight of hidden stairs which wind through the living rock to the wall of the Citadel.' Amana was whispering, as though the awe and sanctity of Kalun somehow made normal speech inappropriate.

'I think I can half remember it.' Dim, shadowy pictures stirred at the back of my mind. Zotala, when had I last spoken to Zotala? A fleeting glimpse of a desperately exhausted old man, staggering through cold rain in an alien November world, was all I could recall clearly. Yet I felt that I had known him well at one time, had sought and followed his advice in older days and stranger times: Zotala, High Priest of the White Magicians of Kalun.

We spent that night just below the storm swept ridge in a shallow rounded shelter, eroded from the rock by centuries of wind and rain. The essence of the Holy City reached us like a subtle perfume. There was peace and protection in it, yet there was power too. It was an awesome place.

At first light we set off down the side of the ridge towards the valley floor that lay between us and the pinnacle of stone on which Kalun was built. Three hours of scrambling descent brought us to something like a goat track which slowly turned into a path. The path had led us to the valley floor by the time the sun was directly overhead, and now we stood staring due west at the column of rock supporting the Citadel.

Kalun seemed to float among the clouds above us, to hover there like some impossible airship.

'How was it built, Lord?' asked Amana. She feared little or nothing, I knew, but as she looked up at the Holy City she moved closer to me and slightly back.

I listened to myself answering her, but I wasn't sure where the words were coming from. They escaped from a hidden depth of memory like cattle escaping from an enclosure when the wall is breached.

'The High Priest, the Lion and the Tiger built Kalun when they first came to Derl Wother, millennia ago. It protected them from the Wild Men and Dark Wizards of the South. The Priest and his Warriors came from beyond the stars in a ship that flew between the worlds. It crashed here and was beyond repair, but some of its wonders could still be used; with power from the broken ship Kalun was raised and secured on the mountain top.'

I shook my head to clear it.

'Did I say that?'

'Yes, Lord, but your voice was strange. It was the voice of the Lion and yet not the voice of the Lion. You seemed to speak across many centuries and from a great distance.'

'What caused it?' I felt disoriented and bewildered.

'The magic of Kalun, Lord. The closer we get, the stronger it becomes. Old secrets of the Holy City call to old memories of lives long past.'

'I think you're right, but it's a weird feeling.'

I seemed to be floating towards the rock pillar rather than walking. Teryn and the three Rangers were following silently

53

as Amana and I crossed the valley floor hand in hand. I was still feeling strange and unreal as we reached the base of the great rock and looked up at the dizzying height. Kalun was surrounded by a strange, warm glow, like soft sunlight seen through mist.

We circled the stone slowly and carefully, looking for the door in the rock that led to the secret stair. We found it on the north side, so finely cut into the stone that its edges looked like black hair against the grey pillar. There was a small depression in the centre of the door, no bigger than a large coin and gleaming at its base like crystal. I stooped to examine it, and suddenly the medallion around my neck began to vibrate gently. Cautiously I held it against the hollow in the door – the vibration increased, became audible, like a shout of friendship and recognition. There was a purposeful whirring from the door and a noise like pneumatic or hydraulic power coming into its own.

The door swung inwards, revealing a dark stair. We stepped over the threshold and began to climb. I went first, with Amana just behind me; Iban came next, then the other two Rangers; Teryn brought up the rear. It was a strange, dark climb inside the weird stone pillar. Some of my terrestrial memories tried to come back but they were faint and remote. This great stone pinnacle reminded me of something I'd seen on earth, but what? The faint earth memories were engulfed by stronger, stranger ones that came from the ancient power of Kalun: a handful of desperate survivors escaping from a cosmic holocaust, millenia ago, motivated by a grim determination to survive. There had been months, years, decades of travel in an ailing ship, limping between the galaxies on a half-crippled ion drive, looping spasmodically in and out of hyperspace.

There had been a difficult landing and a fight to survive in a hostile, alien environment. As I climbed higher, the memories became stronger. Zotala had discovered how to use the life-link: the legend of the Lion, the Tiger and the Priest had been born. The survivors had become feudal war lords, extending their territories ever deeper into the savage slave states of the south, challenging wizards, witches, necromancers and the tyrants of Argath, Kiphol and Ramos . . . This I recalled, but much was still missing.

I was suddenly aware that the stairs had ended on a wide golden landing in front of a translucent circular doorway. The six of us stood silently in front of it for a moment, and then I saw a small circular depression in the centre, similar to the depression which had responded to the medallion before. I stooped and applied the medallion again. Almost immediately the door slid sideways and a warm golden light shone through on to the landing where we stood. A small, dark figure walked quietly towards us.

'I am very glad to see you, my son.'

'Zotala.' I knelt before the High Priest and felt his small, firm hand come to rest on my shoulder.

'Rise up, my son and my brother, Mark Sable of Earth and Black Lion of Dar. You are right welcome in the heart of Kalun and in the heart of Zotala.' He raised each of the party in turn with a firm but gentle hand. 'Amana, my Lioness, we have something in common, have we not? I brought him back from a cold grey world; you brought him back from a tower of fire. I read your love for him in your hands and feet.' Gently he undid the bandages and led her to a basin of golden liquid by the side of a stone seat cut out of the rock wall. He sat her on the stone and knelt at her feet, gently bathing them with the golden liquid. Several of her toes had been burnt to the bone and over these he poured the healing fluid many times.

'Kneel beside me, Amana,' he invited. She joined him by the basin. 'Give me your hands.' With the same great gentleness, Zotala bathed her scarred fingers and the deep burns on her palms. Then he turned and inspected her feet carefully before returning his attention to her hands.

'Mark?'

'Yes, Lord Zotala.'

'I give you back your Lioness. Look at her paws.' He smiled as I took her hands – there were no signs of the grim burns: her hands and feet were as flawless as when I had

55

first rescued her from the Argathians on the dusty road south of Kalaport.

'I am in your debt, Zotala.'

'All men are in debt to their brothers. It is only when we forget those debts that we cease to be men.'

'Thank you, Lord Zotala,' said Amana softly, looking at her hands as though she could not believe they were healed.

'You are most welcome, my daughter and my sister – love-bride of my Black Lion.'

Zotala *knew*. Zotala *understood*. I felt as if his mind *contained* mine and many others, but I did not resent it, for Zotala's understanding was like the understanding of a caring protecting father. He did not seek to control; he never admonished. He was there to help, if, and when, he was needed. Zotala radiated goodness, but his power and wisdom were awe-inspiring. He was the nearest thing I could imagine to an incarnation of a benign god.

He turned and looked steadily at Iban.

'You are welcome here, strong protector of my priests and pilgrims and bane of the Jalnar.' Iban lowered his head in silent appreciation of the High Priest's praise.

'Teryn, the faithful, I have a gift for you.'

'Thank you, Lord Zotala.'

'You are a man of simple faith and strong trust, Teryn, my Ranger. My spirit watched you on the burning tower beside my Lion, and your three hands held the future of Derl Wothor. Let three hands become four.' The old priest took Teryn's wrist and unfastened his hook. 'Gaze at your good hand and imagine its counterpart. Concentrate.' Zotala immersed Teryn's stump in the golden liquid. He held it there, praying over it for a long time. There was an intense, electrical silence in the sacred chamber. The golden liquid began to ripple as though fingers were moving beneath its surface.

'Now, Teryn, behold your gift.' Zotala released the Ranger's arm, and Teryn withdrew his hand from the golden restorative. He stared like a man in a trance at the four perfect fingers and the new thumb.

'Praise the White Gods of Kalun, and bless their Holy Priest,' he whispered, clenching and unclenching his new fist. 'I've been without that hand for twenty years, Lord. I never thought . . . ' Words failed him, but his eyes as they studied his new hand expressed his gratitude and pleasure.

'Now rest and refresh yourselves, sister and brethren, while I speak with my Lion. There is great danger in Derl Wothor. The forces of evil have grown strong while good was exiled. All that is in my house is yours. Go where you will. Eat and drink whatever you choose from my store-rooms.'

Zotala led me along a gleaming, gold-lit metallic passageway into a small, circular room with deeply upholstered benches.

'You remember this room?' It was part question, part statement. I looked round carefully, tugging at my memory as I stared at the walls, the ceiling and the floor.

'I think so . . . but it was part of another life.'

'It was.' He stood up and touched a small panel on the wall. An opaque cover slid back revealing batteries of dials and switches. Their needles flickered occasionally as Zotala's hand brushed them. I studied him as carefully as I had studied the room.

'Our ship,' he said sadly, 'a part of her, at least.'

'Kalun!' I exclaimed suddenly. 'Kalun *was* our ship. You were our leader, Captain, Engineer, Doctor and Scientist . . . The Tiger and I were your guards. We came here together, millenia ago . . . ' Memory suddenly flooded back. I recalled the lost history of my many life-times. Zotala's face was grave when he spoke.

'Our ship contained a co-ordinator sphere, one of the greatest scientific achievements of the world from which we came. It was able to collect, organise, store and apply information like a living mind; but, being a machine, it was without two failings of the living mind: it had no emotional blockages and it forgot nothing. Into that co-ordinator I loaded all the data we brought from our home world, and over the centuries I added all the knowledge of Derl Wothor. That life sphere now encapsulates the living sentience of two planets, hundreds of cultures, millions of minds. Whoever has access to it, and knows how to use it, can control this entire planet and every living thing on its surface. Kalun itself could not withstand an attack based on that knowledge.'

'I think I remember the co-ordinator,' I said, 'it was a glowing crystal sphere about this size.' I held my hands a metre apart.

'That's right. It was kept here, in the old control room – a sort of Holy of Holies.'

'What happened to it?' I asked.

Zotala frowned. 'Kelnos and Andros made a temporary but very dangerous alliance.' My memory clouded. Pictures of the wizards refused to come. It was as though some dark forces were trying to prevent my remembering our enemies. Zotala put a hand on my forehead. 'Fight it, Mark, fight it.' I could feel power flowing in through his hand. My memory cleared again and I saw the Wizards distinctly. Andros of the Swamps was vaguely anthropoid, but he was dark green, saurian and scaly. Taller and heavier than a man, his red eyes glowed malevolently like the eyes of the Jalnar which Iban had slain.

Kelnos the Sand Wizard was a gaunt, scarecrow-like figure whose sparse limbs were wrapped in gauze like the mummified remains of an Egyptian Pharaoh. His eyes were black pits in a muffled face. His hands were bony talons. His feet were like the claws of some weird beast of prey.

'Nearly forty years ago, you, Mark, were an old King and the Tiger was young. The alliance of Kelnos and Andros meant that their nameless horrors, no longer involved in internecine warfare, were free to launch a concerted attack on Kalun. These mountains are riddled with ancient caves and secret tunnels through which the Wizards' armies came. Most of my White Priests were taken by surprise and overwhelmed. For a time the attack was so successful that even I was temporarily driven back, but they could not quite destroy me. I recovered and struck back, driving them from Kalun. Then you arrived leading the cavalry of Dar, and there was terrible slaughter in the valley. We won the battle, but you were killed. One of your knights brought me the sacred medallion, but your life essence had been stolen by Andros and Kelnos. The rest you know.'

'The life-sphere?' I asked.

'When the Wizards first stormed Kalun, I held them at bay for a few moments before I was driven back. During those vital moments a small group of my White Priests escaped with the sphere. They crossed the valley floor and made for the labyrinth of caves below the Rain Mountains, pursued by the nameless horrors of Andros. More than that I could not see, but I *know* they reached the labyrinth.'

'They were not taken?'

'If Andros and Kalnos had the Sphere, they would have attacked me before now. True, their amnesty is long past, and their horrors fight one another again, but if either had the Sphere we should have known it.'

'How do you know your Priests reached the Rain Mountain?'

'Long after the battle, their bodies were found in one of the tunnels. I think they had taken their own lives rather than run the risk of being captured alive and forced to reveal the hiding place of the co-ordinator.'

'Could they have destroyed it, Lord?'

'The Sphere cannot be destroyed unless I destroy it. I alone can unlock the force field which surrounds it.'

I thought long and hard over this paradox. The priests escaped believing their beloved Zotala to be overwhelmed along with their sacred city. Their one thought was to preserve the Sphere from Andros and Kelnos. Desperate, despairing priests, whose world had apparently collapsed around them: where would they run? What would they do with the precious Sphere? To the south lay the heartlands of their enemies. To the east lay the Golden Tiger's land of Valdar. To the north and west lay my cold, wild lands of Dar.

Five rivers rose in the Rain Mountains. The black, un-navigable Abarak ran south between the swamps of Andros and the desert of Kelnos. The Taran flowed through empty lands between my south-western feudatories and the swamps. It emptied into Taran Reach and the Sound of Qua, separating the Forbidden Islands of Qua from the south-western shore of my feudatory. The small, scattered villages did not run as far as the coast; a great barrier forest grew between the cultivated land and the Sound of Qua.

It did not seem likely that the priests would have sent the Sphere south – it was too close to the enemies' territory.

Due west of Kalun the mighty River Dar flowed powerfully into the port of Daris, my own capital city. From there the broad Gulf of Dar, always alive with shipping, emptied into the broad reaches of the Great Western Ocean, where stood Janda, my second city.

The River Aval flowed north, a friendly, much crossed boundary between my land and the Tiger's Kingdom of Valdar. The Aval emptied into the Bay of Valdar at the edge of the frozen regions of the north. Its great port, Valdaris, was often ice-locked in winter when the Northern Ocean froze over for months at a time.

The fifth river was the Kala, running past Kalaford to Kalaport. Had the priests committed the Sphere to one of the rivers? Had they buried it in the labyrinth?

'If our people had found it, they would have brought it to me, or sent me word,' said Zotala. 'If the Wizards had it, they would have moved against me by now. So it must be lost or unrecognised. It has been missing for close on forty years, and with each day that passes I fear it may fall into the hands of the Wizards or the League of Three Cities. Imagine the tyrants of Argath wielding the power of the Sphere.' Zotala shuddered. 'So that is your first task, Mark. Find the Sphere for me, and bring it back to Kalun.'

'There is another task, Lord?'

'Perhaps it is the second part of the first one, for I feel they are bound up together. My other son, your King-Brother the Golden Tiger is old, and I fear for his safety. They must not capture his life essence as they once captured yours. It takes all three of us to hold the power of evil in check.'

60

'Where is the Tiger?'

'He led the army of Valdar south, to search the desert and the swamps for the Sphere. He was always raiding the enemies' lands. I warned him that his forces were too few . . .' Zotala smiled, 'but he is a stubborn old man, and he would not listen.'

'Why did he think the Sphere had gone south?'

'He dreamed a dream in which the sun rose in the south, a crystal sun sinking slowly from the air to the land. It called to him, "come to me and find your heart's desire, but come swiftly lest another find me first and make the lands grow dark." '

'And there has been no word of him?'

'Word travels slowly here, Mark, but there has been none for many months.'

'Then I must find him, but I need to raise armies first, men enough to cut their way through swamps and deserts.'

'You are wise.' A troubled look crossed his face. 'The path ahead of you is not an easy one; parts of it are dark, but I see brightness at its end.'

We rejoined the others. I ate wholemeal bread spread with honey, for the bees of Kalun are famous for the nectar they bring home from the sweet white mountain flowers. I drank goats' milk and Zotala's home made wine before we set out westwards towards Daris.

Chapter Seven

The Armies of Dar

The upper reaches of the River Dar were beautiful as we followed a well worn mountain track from the Rain Mountain towards Daris. Every few yards tiny paths ran from the main track to the grey stone faces of the mountains themselves, and I realised as we passed that these tracks led to the ancestral tombs of the citizens of Daris. Each ancient family had its own spacious burial chamber among the catacombs and holy caves of these western slopes. No evil beasts of Andros found any lasting refuge among the honoured dead of Daris. Their descendants, believing that their reincarnated ancestors lived again among them, paid homage to the dead and kept the tombs fresh and clean. The heraldic devices of the old families, unchanged for generations, were cut into the rocks above the tomb entrances and on to the great stones that sealed them. Here we passed a war horse rearing on its hind legs; there was a pick and spade: here an anchor was cut; nearby was a wheel; above it the outline of an axe was clearly marked. A hand, a trident, a rose, a plough, a crescent moon: all were there in the rock tombs, and many others beside. Flowers twined into wreaths, and small symbolic gifts of food and wine also lay at the tomb entrances. Before one tomb a rusting sword had long ago been thrust into the stony soil by the widow of an old soldier who had left no son to bear it after he died. On a sudden impulse I drew the ancient blade from the stone scabbard which had held it for so long, and spoke to the door of the ancient tomb.

'Old warrior of Dar, your sword is drawn again. The armies of Dar ride south to seek the Tiger King who is lost. The spirit that once animated the dust within this tomb may ride again with us, clothed in strong new flesh and wielding a sword on which there is no rust. Long ago you drew this sword in my service. I draw it now to honour your memory, and replace it again as a sign of your resting place.'

We continued our journey, but the tomb with the rusting sword troubled me. Amana's grip on my hand was sensitive and perceptive.

'You knew him, Lord; I sense it.' She looked suddenly at the distant horizon. 'That sword shall be drawn in your service again, Lord, in time of great need.'

'Your visit to Kalun has made you a seer,' I smiled.

'No one can meet Zotala or enter his citadel without being changed. There hatred withers, and lovers are welded together like molten gold. The blind see; the lame walk, and the sick are made whole.' She looked at her hands again, and glanced across at Teryn. He became aware of her gaze and smiled back at her.

'And memories are restored,' I said, 'at least in part.' We walked on together in deep, thoughtful silence.

'Tasks are given?' she suggested.

'And gladly accepted,' I replied, 'to find the Sphere of Power and to rescue my King-Brother the Golden Tiger of Valdar.'

Around the next corner we saw the roofs of Daris gleaming in the sun, shining after a recent shower from the Great Western Ocean, a shower that had not yet reached the tomb slopes where we now walked.

'Shall I signal to the city, Lord?' asked Teryn. I nodded and called a halt while the Ranger unslung his polished shield and held it up to catch the sun. He directed its bright reflection to an open space in the centre of the distant city. A

63

moment later I saw a series of tiny answering flashes. Teryn replaced his shield and we walked on again.

The tomb track joined a small road which in turn joined a broader one a mile or two farther along.

Daris was still about an hour's march ahead when I heard the first jubilant peal of bells and the sound of a great gong being struck over and over again.

Another mile, and as we rounded a bend in the road there was a cheer from the thin beginning of a crowd that lined the rest of the route from here to the city, growing deeper as we approached.

'Hail to the Black Lion, Lord of Dar.'

'Long live the King.'

It was like a mediaeval pageant. The citizens of Daris were out in force, some in their brightly coloured festive costumes, others in workaday leather where they had suddenly left their benches and come out to join the cheering, welcoming throng.

I enjoyed the warm loyalty of my people to the full. I acknowledged their cheering with a smile; I waved back to the jubilant crowd; I lifted Amana on to my shoulder so that my people could see their new queen and share my joy in her; I put my free hand on the heads and shoulders of cheering children as we strode into the city. I clasped the hands of their delighted parents, and saluted their dignified grey-haired grandparents. This was my city and I had been absent for forty years. The oldest citizens had been young or middle aged when I had been taken from them. The young men and women, and the excited children, had seen me only in pictures and statues: now their king was home. Why should they not cheer, and why should I not enjoy their welcome? There was too much sorrow and danger in the world; happiness should be enjoyed, savoured and prolonged as far as possible.

'Do you remember your palace, Lord?' A gorgeously robed old herald with a ceremonial banner in his hands stood beside me, to usher us into the Royal Palace of Daris.

I followed him from room to room, half-discovering and

half-remembering the royal treasures. Glorious, ornate tapestries recalling past wars and ancient battles, hung on the walls of every great hall and formal chamber. There were dancing rooms, music rooms, games rooms, art galleries, courtyards with orchards, flowers and fountains, stables of magnificent horses, great stores of weapons and armour, wardrobes of rich robes, treasuries bulging with jewels and gleaming coins – a palace such as a king might truly dream of.

Memory groped for a name to go with the old herald's face. He had been young when I had last seen him. The long grey hair had been as black and glossy as a raven's wing. The broad shoulders had not been bowed.

'Korinus,' I said at last, 'my chief Herald and Steward. Have you kept all in readiness for so long? It is as though I had but left this morning for a day's hunting.'

Korinus straightened his old shoulders a little and stood a fraction taller.

'I have said every morning, Lord, "*The Lion may return today*," and I have held everything ready for your home-coming at any hour of the day or night. Behold your throne, my Lord.'

At a signal from Korinus a dozen heralds formed up on each side of the throne room and blew a jubilant royal fanfare. I strode down that avenue of magnificent sound, with Amana on my left arm and mounted the great black marble throne over which a life sized gilded lion was carved in bas relief on the wall. There was no other throne, and I took Amana on my knee.

'Korinus,' I ordered, 'most honoured of the faithful Stewards of Dar, let a throne of white marble be brought for Queen Amana and set forever on the left of the throne of the Lion.'

'It shall be done, my Lord; the most skilful of your palace Masons shall carve it from the royal quarries. They shall work without rest until it is in place.'

'Korinus.'

'Yes, Lord.'

5

'Send your heralds to my captains in every corner of the kingdom. We raise an army this day to rescue my King-Brother, the Golden Tiger.' The old man's eyes lit up with excitement.

'Truly the Lion is home,' he cried. 'It shall be done, Lord, at once.'

I learned afterwards that the basis of Korinus's whole organisation was simple trust and complete delegation. In Dar duty was sacred, and a royal or feudal order was carried out not as an obligation but as a matter of pride and honour.

The social structure was a simple pyramid as far as orders were concerned, but a family, or brotherhood, in terms of social welfare. A soldier of Dar went ungrudgingly to fight knowing that his family's standard of living would not be affected by his death. A royal messenger left his harvest ungathered, knowing his neighbours would reap and store it faithfully while he rode on a royal assignment. A mason would cut and carve stone for the palace knowing that his brothers in the craft were taking care that his home workshop was not neglected.

The children of Dar matured early and were given as much responsibility as they were ready to take. It was no strange thing to find ten year olds ploughing, driving flocks and herds, or selling goods in the market places. The old grew old at their own pace; there was no social pressure on them to relinquish jobs they enjoyed; there were no artificial age barriers to deprive a Darian of status. A Darian could be nine or ninety – if he did a man's work his peers naturally regarded him as a man.

Regor, one of the most skilled masons, had supervised the nonstop work on the new white throne. It had been installed only that morning and Amana sat beside me now as we looked together at the assembled war lords of Dar.

There were leaders of well trained citizens militias from Daris and Janda, each with their distinctive tunics, sturdy farm workers and herdsmen from the cultivated land between the two great cities. Boatmen's leaders from the friendly banks of the Aval, workers from the small water-powered manufacturing towns along its banks; even the first few captains from distant Valdaris, the Tiger's City, had made their way swiftly up the Aval to join the muster.

Standing at the back of the hall were leaders of the northern tribes, thick-set nomadic hunters of the cold plains, and bearded woodsmen from the logging camps of the coniferous forests – hard to distinguish from the bears they had to fight.

From Nestor, south of the great Gulf of Dar, the loyal captains of my Northern Feudatory had ridden, accompanied by the nearer village lords from the Feudatory's manorial estates.

Korinus struck the great gong, and, after its powerful tone had died away, there was silence in the throne room.

'Soldiers,' I began, 'Captains of the Twin Kingdoms, and Loyal Allies from the Feudatories, I have called this muster to accomplish two great tasks for the Lord Zotala, High Priest of Holy Kalun.' I paused. 'My King-Brother, the Golden Tiger, led some of the army of Valdar south to the desert and the swamps. Perhaps he yet lives. If he does we will rescue him. If he is dead, we will bring his body home for burial with royal honour in Valdaris.' I paused again. 'Yet there is another task even more important than this: the recovery of the great crystal sphere of Zotala. If it falls into the hands of Kelnos the Cruel or Andros the Accursed, all of Derl Wothor will be in peril. Already the sphere has been missing for too long. It must be found and returned to Zotala for safe keeping.' There were nods and murmurs of approval from the assembled soldiers who held both Zotala and the Tiger in high esteem.

'What is your plan, Lord?' asked a leather-clad northerner, a grizzled veteran carrying a heavy two-handed axe.

'To travel south through the empty lands west of the River Taran, making raids into the swamps of Abarak as we go and interrogating the swamp dwellers. Scouts will also search the forests west of the empty lands of Taran, and ask the woodsmen and charcoal burners for news. Then we will cross the Taran and follow the eastern bank around the coast as far as Taran Reach and the Sound of Qua. The coastal route will take us east, then north to the Pirate City of Barak. The corsairs will have the choice of giving us free passage and answering our questions, or being wiped out. I think they will give us passage.' Several of my captains were smiling grimly.

'I'd rather they didn't, Lord; I have an old score to settle in Barak,' said a tall, deeply-tanned countryman from the Southern Feudatory. There were murmurs of assent.

'So be it,' I said. 'Reparation and free passage, or total destruction. That is the choice we give Barak.' There was another brief pause, and then I continued. 'From Barak we head north through the deserted lands east of the Abarak, striking west across the swamps and east across the desert. Somewhere, somehow we shall find a prisoner who knows something of the Tiger. If we have discovered nothing by the time we reach the Eastern Feudatory, just below the River Kala, we strike east, and replenish our supplies in Kalaport. From Kalaport we go south to Argath – perhaps the League of Three Cities has knowledge of the Tiger.'

'When do we march, Lord?' asked one of the Captains of Valdar, anxious to find his king.

'At sunrise, the day after tomorrow. Men of Dar and Valdar, with those from the far north, will set out with me from Daris. Men of the Northern and Southern Feudatories, Militia from Nestor and Thosan, will move as soon as they are ready and join the main army by the banks of the Taran.'

A sudden sharp cry pierced the hall. I turned in the direction of the sound.

'Beware, Lord! There is triumph and glory for the armies of Dar and their allies, but there is darkness and peril for the Lion who leads them.' It was Conos, the Blind Seer of Daris, who called out. 'Yet brightness and glory shall come again to you when all hope is gone. On the other side of that which is worse than death, that which is better than life shall be restored. Lord, when you are in the deepest pit and ready to die, remember the words of Conos and live.'

68

The Blind Seer's prophecy troubled me: it was so similar to Zotala's words. What did it mean? Whatever it meant, I had to go on. The armies of Dar could not be mustered without one of their Kings.

Chapter Eight

The Swamps of Abarak

Three city bridges cross the broad, deep waters of the River Dar. The highest upstream is the smallest, and it leads to a road that winds towards Kalun, and then beyond the Rain Mountains to the Eastern Feudatory. The central bridge is the oldest – it led once to the busy water traffic of the Taran river – but now it leads only to the empty lands. The bridge nearest to the sea is the biggest, and it leads to the great high road linking Daris with Nestor in the west and Thosan in the south. My army crossed the old central bridge and headed due south for the empty lands on the north-western banks of the sluggish Taran at the edge of the swamps.

A warm mist rose from the marshes as we marched about a mile to the west of the river bank. Darian priests and healers averred that the brackish waters of the Taran, and the vapours from the foul swamps of Abarak beyond it, carried fever and plague. Even a mile away, the decaying smell of the sluggish water brought with it the threat of disease and death. It was often said in Dar that more men were killed by the swamps than by the nameless horrors who served Andros.

I called a dozen of the senior captains to me as the late afternoon sun began heading for the western horizon.

'We will make our first raids across the Taran now, with

the setting sun behind us and its light in the eyes of our enemies. These strange creatures of the darkness cannot easily face the sunlight – it hinders and frightens them. Remember, we want information: capture anything that can talk.' I allocated areas of the river to each captain, and, taking Amana with me, I led the most southern raid myself.

The armies of Dar were well equipped. Each company had its own small portable boats – ideal for raids such as these. We paddled silently across the unwholesome river and drew the boats up safely on the muddy banks of the fetid swamp beyond. Picking our way carefully through the marsh was a slow and laborious business, and time was against us. In the hour of daylight that remained we had to locate as many swamp-dwellers as we could capture alive and get them back to the empty lands for interrogation. To have started earlier would have been to lose the tactical advantage of the low sunlight; to have started later would have been to risk being caught in the swamps after the sun had set.

I vaguely recalled some of the Darian folk-tales of the wer-beasts and half-human things that lived among the marshes. Grey-green and slimy they were, web-footed and sharp clawed. The legends told of beasts the size of a house with long necks and serpents' heads: things that drank blood and ate human flesh. There were sinister stories of plants with sucking mouths and tough, fast-moving tendrils that twined around unwary travellers, dragging them down to death below the choking mud.

Amana too had heard the legends, for she stayed close to my side as we crossed the marshes in search of some sign of life. From time to time I looked at the position of the setting sun.

'We shall have to turn back soon,' I said quietly, 'with or without prisoners.' Even as I spoke, there was an urgent splashing sound from behind a tall clump of sickly green swamp grass. A weird, lizard-like creature, about half the height of a man, broke cover and darted swiftly away from us. He would easily have outrun a swift-footed native Darian, but my legs, trained in the high, muscle-building gravity of

71

earth, were too fast for him. I caught him by the back of the neck before he had covered ten metres and hauled him, squealing shrilly, clear of the wet ground. He was slippery and hard to hold, but Amana had cords around his limbs in seconds. He snapped viciously and clawed wildly as we tied him. His shrill squeals changed to harsh, angry, deep-throated growls as I hefted him to one shoulder and turned back westwards. Amana signalled to our men to retrace their steps, and we crossed the river again without incident. After roll call, I checked the prisoners, and found we had seven in all: the lizard man I had caught; a creature covered in long grey fronds who looked like a walking willow tree; a multi-legged, broad-footed beast; a huge, scaly anthropoid, over seven feet tall, with glaring, hostile eyes, a sloping, bone-ridged forehead and webbed hands and feet; something with flippers that looked like a medieval artist's impression of a walrus or sea-lion; and two spindly-limbed little horrors with bright black eyes and needle sharp fangs who looked as though they were equipped to prey on tiny fish and am-phibians. Looking at this motley assortment, I had no way of knowing whether any of them could either think or com-municate, but we had to start somewhere. The Golden Tiger and the Life Sphere were missing. The Tiger had been head-ing for Abarak. These things were swamp dwellers, and, as such, were closer to the grim secrets of Abarak than most other inhabitants of Derl Wothor. I intended to know all they knew before the night was over.

I called for interpreters and five of my soldiers came for-ward to help with the long night's work. These five were all familiar with the languages of Abarak to some degree. Two had been neophyte priests at Kalun, and, as such, had studied many of the strange tongues of Derl Wothor. The White Priests who served Zotala often went far and wide as envoys or missionaries, and languages formed an essential part of their training. After a year or so training in Kalun, however, these two young Darians had decided that the priesthood was not for them and had returned to their homes in the Northern Feudatory. The other three interpreters were ex-merchant seamen, brothers who had been captured by the corsairs of Barak Bay, destined for the slave mines of Argath, shipwrecked en route and miraculously rescued by a passing Valdarian ship.

During their captivity in Barak they had had some contact with swamp dwellers and learnt a little of their language.

After an hour's patient interrogation, we judged that the lizard-man, the walking tree and the scaly giant could probably communicate if they wanted to; we were certain that the multi-legged beast could not and neither could the thing like a walrus. The real puzzles were the vicious, spindly limbed swamp rodents. They made high-pitched squeaking sounds alternating with harsh guttural growls, but it was almost impossible to tell whether these were simply expressive animal calls or true speech patterns.

Teryn looked at the little horrors without much enthusiasm. 'Kill them, Lord,' he said simply. 'Keep these three,' he indicated the probable talkers, 'and let these two go.' He pointed without animosity to the walrus-like object and the thing with too many broad-footed legs.

'I'm inclined to agree,' I said slowly. 'I don't like the look of these at all.' I pointed to the thin-limbed, needle-toothed marsh rodents.

'I think I've seen something like them before, Lord,' said Quarl, the younger of the two ex-priests, 'preserved in the museum laboratories at Kalun. Lord Zotala pointed them out to our group, but I can't recall exactly what he said. He didn't like them and said they were more dangerous than they looked . . . '

Four bright black eyes regarded Quarl as the swamp rodents turned their heads menacingly towards him. Thin grey lips drew back across the startling whiteness of the teeth. They tugged and snapped at the leather thongs with which we had secured them. Quarl drew back a little as they hissed and snapped. I drew my sword and held the point close to their angry mouths. They snapped and clawed at the steel for a few seconds, then quietened.

'Try to remember, Quarl.' He closed his eyes, and furrowed his brow in deep concentration.

'Lord Zotala said they were sent out by Andros. They are creatures of the wizard!' He was shouting excitedly. 'Look at their eyes, Lord, for they are the eyes of Andros . . .'

The bright, black, rodent eyes were changing, turning red and becoming translucent. It was as though something powerful and dangerous far away was peering out through them. The tiny bodies surged with power. Thongs snapped like paper.

'Kill them, Lord,' screamed Quarl. He was terrified of the strangely changed creatures. My sword spitted one from mouth to tail as it leapt for my face. Teryn's dagger sliced the other in half in mid-flight as it flew at Quarl. Thin black blood dripped from the tiny corpses. It smoked and smelled foul. The bodies continued to twitch.

'Burn them,' I ordered.

The death of Andros's rodents had a powerful effect on the remaining prisoners. The giant spoke gruffly to Quarl who had now regained his composure.

'He says that Andros will be angry at the death of his servants. He will send his creatures against us and destroy us. He says if we are wise we will run for our lives.' The giant looked contemptuously at the soldiers around him, and grunted again.

'He says we are puny; Andros will devour us.' Wild anger from the remote barbarian past surged through me.

'Cut him loose and give him a sword.'

Even Teryn moved away from me. The battle fury was almost tangible, radiating from me in violent, black waves. The scaly giant seemed to shrink a little as he stared at me with the hostile eyes below their bony ridges.

Like a man approaching a volcano, Teryn edged nearer again and handed the giant a long, two-handed Darian cavalry sword. The monster sliced through the thongs that had secured it and flexed one arm experimentally, trying the weight and balance of the heavy steel.

Slowly and deliberately I unstrapped my armour and took

74

off my helmet. I unbuckled the sword belt and threw my dagger into the firm soil.

'Quarl.'

'Yes, Lord.' His voice was a whisper.

'Tell this swamp spawn that he is nothing, less than nothing; I scorn and despise him; I need no weapons to fight such as he. Tell him the Black Lion has returned to destroy Andros and all his followers.'

As Quarl finished interpreting the giant roared – a mixture of fear and anger – and swung the sword. I leapt over it and smashed a rock-hard fist into the side of his scaly head. The eyes began to glaze and the great knees buckled. I tore the sword from his sagging fingers and flung it away. Another explosive punch, this time to the body, sent green scales flying and bent the giant double. My knee came up to meet the bony ridges as his head came down. He straightened up with a jerk and crashed backwards, but I had him by the throat almost as soon as he hit the ground. The scaly green flesh began to collapse under my fingers.

'Stop, Lord, oh please stop!' Gentle hands closed over my wrists as I crushed the giant's throat into oblivion. Only Amana would have dared. I let go of the broken swamp giant and stood up.

'Tie him up. I'll question him later.' I turned questioningly to Amana. 'Why did you stop me? Did you pity the creature?'

'No, Lord, but we need information from him. You have already broken his mind and body. When he recovers consciousness he will tell you all he knows. Dead, he could tell us nothing. Your grip when you are angry crushes rock into dust; a moment more and you would have torn his head from his shoulders.'

'Spoken like a warrior queen.'

'Let us eat and drink, while he recovers, Lord. Then the prisoners will talk – I know it.'

I washed and put on a clean tunic. We ate savoury vegetable broth, roasted fowl and a dish of fruit. I emptied half a flagon of sweet red wine, and felt almost human again. I went back to the prisoners. One of my Darian army surgeons was examining the giant.

'You've dented his skull in two places, broken four of his ribs and cracked the shoulder he landed on, Lord,' said the surgeon.

'Can he talk?'

'He says he would lead us to Andros's castle rather than fight the Black Lion again,' said Quarl.

Chapter Nine

The Prisoner's Tale

'Lord, he craves mercy and promises to answer all your questions in return for his life and freedom,' said Quarl. The scaly giant trembled as I approached.

'Tell him he's in no position to make bargains. If I'm satisfied with the answers, he'll live. If I like what I hear, he'll go free.' Quarl interpreted. The scaly hands shook as the giant listened.

'Find out his name.'

'He is called Orthos, Lord.'

'His tribe, his people?'

'He says he has no tribe, Lord; he was *made* in the castle of Andros like the others.'

'Ask about the others.'

Teryn sent for military scribes to take down the giant's description of Andros's creations. It was a long, slow process, interesting in some parts, revolting in others. Andros had built up quite a collection. The Wizard certainly did not lack imagination. There were swamp serpents of every size and colour, venomous to various degrees. There were lizards and things that crawled on wide webs over the soft marshy ground. There were small, vicious rodents that could infiltrate into secret places to watch and listen – the eyes and ears of Andros. The pair which Teryn and I had disposed

77

of were samples of that breed, but there were several different varieties. Andros had also experimented with crawling predatory mudfish, poisonous insects that swarmed at his command, carnivorous plants, gigantic leeches and gliding lizards that swooped from the shade of the dark trees edging the swamp.

The scribes would circulate this information to the captains, and soon every soldier in my army would know about the strengths and weaknesses of his enemies. Sword and axe were the mainstay of the soldiers of Dar, but we also had military engineers to devise and create new weapons for specific purposes. Our artificers knew the secret of flying fire that could be deployed in clouds of deadly flame against poisonous insects. Our armourers could forge barbed tridents for transfixing the necks of things that crawled across mud. Traditional blades could soon be curved and adapted for severing the stems and slashing the encircling tendrils of carnivorous plants.

It was only when Orthos had exhausted his catalogue of Andros's horrors that I questioned him about the Golden Tiger and the crystal sphere; his ignorance of both seemed genuine.

The miniature lizard-man whom I had seized confirmed much of what Orthos had revealed about Andros's creations, but he, too, pleaded ignorance about the heart of my quest.

With deeply discerning intuition, Amana suggested that we should take the tree-man away from the others. He alone of the captives had shown us no hostility, and, despite his odd appearance, I had the feeling that he was a *natural*, evolutionary being, rather than one of Andros's artifacts.

As soon as we were clear of the prisoners, he sprang his first surprise.

'You may send Quarl and the other interpreters to their tents if you wish, Lord,' he said in perfect Darian.

'I knew he was not like the others,' said Amana excitedly.

'Who are you?' I asked him.

'My name in the old speech is Nyrblos, and I lived at the edge of the Taran long before the empty lands were deserted.

I was established here when Andros came blighting the soil and polluting the river. I was old before Zotala crossed the galaxies. I knew the Lion and the Tiger when they were simple guardsmen in Zotala's house during their first incarnation. I do not often concern myself with wizards and warlords, for they are as passing sparks when the night fire burns by the river.'

'How then did my men capture you?' I asked.

'They did not capture me. I wished to speak with you, and it amused me to play at being swamp spawn for a spell.'

'Is this your real form?' asked Amana, pointing to one of the long willowy fronds that grew from Nyrblos's head.

'My remote ancestors had permanent shape, and this shape you now see resembles it somewhat; I have been able to change my form at will for several millennia.' There was a sudden rustling and the crackle of energy being released. The air smelled like summer rain. Nyrblos had gone, but Amana now stood on my right *and my left*. There was another rustle and a second soft energy discharge. One Amana vanished and I stood looking at a tall, powerfully built man. He was over six feet and his short curly hair was as black as jet. His face was strong, proud and disconcertingly familiar. He laughed suddenly and vanished. The fronded tree shape of Nyrblos reappeared.

'Lord,' gasped Amana, 'there were two of you.'

'And there were two of you,' I answered.

'It will be simpler if I stay as I am. This is an old and comfortable shape,' said Nyrblos from below his fronds, 'and I wear it like a garment that an old man loves because he wore it when he was young.'

'Nyrblos, with such power you could help me to destroy the wizards and bring peace to Derl Wothor.'

'You speak too simply, Black Lion. Life is not like that. There are some things worse than war and others which are better than peace. You think of yourself and your cause as *"good"* and of Andros and Kelnos as *"evil"*, but these words are misused and misunderstood. You see only black and white in a universe full of grey. You yourself have done much that others would call *evil*, but your followers regard you as a *good* king, and rightly so, for your rule is kinder than the rule of wizards. Yet, given an infinity of time and space in which to search for comparisons, there are rulers beside whom you are evil, and others beside whom the wizards are benign.'

Amana shook her head angrily. 'I cannot accept that.' She flung her arms around me protectively. 'He *is* good. No king could be better . . . No man could be better.' Nyrblos rustled his fronds before speaking.

'You see with eyes of love, and some philosophers aver that love is blind; yet, in a sense, love sees more truly than wisdom. For you, Amana, there could be no better man, and for him no better woman. For you, personal truth is more significant than universal truth. We do not live in the universe, we live in our own personalities.'

'Nyrblos,' I broke in, 'if I understand you correctly, the ancient war between the King Brothers and the Wizards is as nothing to your life span. You are older even than Zotala?'

'Far older,' he agreed.

'You do not regard our wars as serious?'

'I did not say that. I do not regard them as seriously as you do, which is not to say that I do not regard them at all. A man farms his land for fifty years; one year wolves fight stags on the edge of his field, and some of his crops are trodden in the battle. The man has a purpose – growing wheat – which is not significant to wolves or deer. The animals have a purpose which is not significant to the farmer. Yet almost by accident, the actions of one have affected the designs of another. It is then that the farmer emerges from his isolation and considers the ways of wolves and stags.'

'Have I damaged your crops?'

'No, it is Andros who disturbs my swamps and their inhabitants. And I have not yet decided what to do about him.' He paused and there was a prolonged rustling of fronds. 'Perhaps I was less than just to you earlier. When you are very old and see too many shades of grey perhaps it is easy to forget that light grey is almost white and dark grey is nearly black. Too much toleration leads to as many errors as prejudice.'

'Then you will help us against the Wizards?' asked Amana, starting forward eagerly.

'For a little while only, though it may seem longer to you. I will warn you of peril where I see it, and I will teach you how to summon me in time of need. It would be against my interests too for your co-ordinator to fall into the hands of the wizards; unfortunately, I don't know where it is, though I have an inkling of where it may have been. Neither can I locate the Golden Tiger, though I sense that he is alive.' He reached out a bunch of fronds and touched us both. There was a mild tingling like an electric shock, and I knew I was closer to Amana than I had ever been before. It was as though our minds were in direct contact, as though we could understand each other's thoughts and feelings without the intermediary of speech or gesture. We were each other and Nyrblos was the medium in which we lived our united life. He withdrew his fronds and the sensation ended.

'I see danger for you,' he said reluctantly, 'sorrow and darkness, a despair that is worse than death. Zotala sensed it; so did Conos. After the darkness a great light shines, and after the despair there is glory and joy. You must believe it, Mark, or else the despair will destroy you – and, if you fall, your Kingdom will fall. You are very strong, Black Lion of Dar, but many depend upon your strength and courage and you must not fail them. There are greater Gods than the Gods of Kalun; there are Beings older than I. Nothing happens by chance in this universe. The wolf is a passing shadow to the farmer but the farmer is a passing shadow to the field. The field itself is a passing shadow to the planet. We have powers and gifts to accomplish certain tasks, but success or failure lies within ourselves. The *will* is ours. Think well, Mark, and remember my words. A strong arm wields a sword, but a strong heart wields an empire.'

'Go on, Nyrblos, go on,' I urged.

'If I knew more, I would say more. I see whole ages of the past but only broken fragments of future moments. The past is done, rolled out like a great woven cloth. The future is not made yet. I see where two or three threads may cross; I see

6

the outline of the stitching they may form together, but each separate thread lives, has its own will and is, therefore, unpredictable.'

His fronds moved swiftly together, and he handed each of us a small heavy metal disc, like a silver coin.

'This is how you may summon me in time of need: although I do not guarantee that I shall be in range of your distress call. If I am, I shall do my best to answer.'

'How is it used?' asked Amana.

'Place it in the palm of one hand and press the other palm against it. Think of me as you do it. If I am receiving the signal you will feel the same tingling you felt when I touched you. Try it.'

We pressed the coins as he had told us, and immediately felt the electrical vibrations.

'There is no theoretical limit to their range, but certain substances muffle or block the signal. A deep dungeon is a poor location for a transmitter, a mountain top or the roof of a building is a good location. Strong emotion boosts the signal, and, as I trust you not to disturb me without good cause, you will be experiencing strong emotion when you do call for aid.'

'Nyrblos . . . ' I began but there was a sudden crackling discharge of energy and an extra soldier of Dar stood in the group. The unknown soldier melted into the crowd with a wave of his hand, and was gone.

Under cover of darkness in the early hours of the morning we released the giant and the man-lizard into the turgid waters of the Taran. At first light we breakfasted, broke camp and headed south again. We had learnt little or nothing of the Tiger and the crystal globe, but we had learnt much that was useful. Even under adverse conditions the men of Dar marched fast. They were still fresh and fit. Morale was high and food was good and plentiful. We had covered over thirty miles before making another sortie across the dark river.

My force was again farthest to the south when we crossed. We had set strong guards around the perimeter of the camp because the trees of the boundary forest of the Northern Feudatory now lay to the west of us, between our camp and my feudal city of Nestor. A cunning enemy could have come through that belt of forest and attacked us from the west. The night before there had been no forest between us and friendly territory, the enemy had lain across the river.

In the distance I saw the stark outline of a ruined castle. Vines and creepers had overgrown parts of it, but in many places the black stone was still visible.

'There are legends of wer-beasts, Lord,' said a young Darian anxiously.

'They bleed when they're cut,' I said grimly. Amana undid the leather bag she carried and produced a small, jewelled dagger with a bright silver blade.

'The wise man in Kalaford once said that a silver blade is deadly to a wer-beast,' she said.

'I too have heard that silver is poisonous to them,' I agreed, 'but I have not seen one – at least, I cannot recall having seen one.'

'I have, Lord.' It was Teryn who spoke.

'What are they like, Teryn?' asked Amana.

'The one I saw was distant, and running fast through shadowy moonlight, but I prayed to Kalun all the same.'

'What manner of thing was it?' persisted Amana.

'About the height of a man and covered in coarse dark hair. The face was like the face of an ape, or a bear. I saw moonlight on the teeth as it ran. The front limbs were thick and powerful ending in glittering claws.'

'The wise man of Kalaford said the wer-beasts lived among the ruins of Abarak,' said Amana.

'In all the tales I've heard,' said the young soldier beside us, 'they live in ruins.'

The remains of the castle seemed strange and sinister as we approached them. Windows stared like sightless eyes in a dead, broken face. The creeping vines moved a little – the last few strands of hair on the skull of an ancient corpse.

'We'll search it carefully,' I ordered, 'in twos or fours. No man is to enter any part of it alone.'

There was a sinister atmosphere inside the crumbling stone, as though the dark walls still clung to memories of nameless atrocities long forgotten in the outside world. Amana and I found a flight of slime-stained stairs in the corner of a chamber below the surface of the marsh and descended carefully. Surprisingly, the stairs were better preserved than much of the upper storeys, and although they were damp and slippery they seemed firmly set.

'Let go,' I shouted suddenly, releasing her hand as though it were red hot. The stair on which I was treading had given way completely and without warning – a carefully engineered trap, still working after countless centuries. As I released her she flung herself back up the steps and clutched wildly for a hold on the slippery stones. For a second she swayed dangerously on the brink of the pit into which I had plunged; then her hands got a grip, and she regained her balance.

'Lord, are you hurt?' I could see her silhouette as she peered anxiously over the treacherous stone. After a fall of about three metres I had landed on my feet in what felt like mud.

'I'm all right,' I shouted back. 'I landed on something soft.' My voice echoed strangely in the stone pit. Another silhouette appeared at the top of the trap. It was Teryn.

'I heard you calling, Lord. I've sent men for ropes; they won't take long.'

'Well done, Teryn . . . ' I began, then stopped in mid-sentence – *the floor was moving beneath me.* It had tilted sideways and the angle was increasing. The mud which had broken my fall now prevented my getting a grip on the sloping floor. I groped wildly for a hold, but there was only treacherous mud and the smooth wet stone beneath it.

'The floor's moving,' I roared, 'I'm sliding down it!' I heard Teryn shouting orders. There was a flurry of activity at the mouth of the trap. The Ranger was making a human chain to try to reach me, but it was too late. The floor had now tilted over forty degrees, and, like a shark floundering in the shallows, I was sliding away into unknown depths. There was a desperate cry and a heavy splash. Amana landed just

84

above me. She had *jumped* from the steps into the pit. Our arms locked in a flurry of mud and darkness as the tilting increased, and we slithered deeper and deeper into the unknown horror below.

The wild slide ended in a great quagmire of mud and silt at the bottom of the sloping shaft. We struggled waist deep in the pouring mud and fought our way clear of the avalanche of slime that was still pouring down the shaft. Teryn's voice was just audible above the sound of the rushing mud. Then there was the sound of grinding metal and stone, and Teryn's voice was cut off by some great barrier.

'Lord,' said Amana quietly, 'Lord, we are buried alive.'

'Alive,' I repeated, 'still alive, and together.' I hugged her through the thick layer of mud that covered us both. 'You jumped.' I tried to sound angry, but my heart sang and the song reached my voice. 'Jumped,' I said again, disbelievingly, and yet I was not really surprised. Her leap into the darkness behind me had been inevitable once she had realised I could not climb back. It was part of her, like climbing the tower, or running her heart out to raise the fishermen's militia at Kalaport.

'Lord, you would have jumped also.'

'Into the chasm between the worlds, if you were there.' Gently I scraped the mud from her cheeks and lips, took her tightly in my arms and kissed her, there, in the stygian darkness below the swamps. In the warmth of her kisses I found my strength and courage again.

'We can't get out the way we came in,' I said decisively. 'We must go forward.'

'Yes, Lord.' Hand in hand we set out together into the darkness.

Chapter Ten

The Sphere

Our sense of touch told us we were in some sort of tunnel or passageway. I could feel the roof when I stretched a hand above my head, and the walls were within reach of our fingertips when we walked side by side. It was a gloomy and terrible place, mud and water ran beneath our feet, and I soon realised from the direction of the flow that the tunnel was going deeper below the marsh. After a time the water was knee deep; then we were wading. Another hundred metres and Amana was clinging to my shoulders as I strode through water that swirled around my armpits. Fifty metres more and I was swimming while she clung to me. It was not long before I felt the roof of the tunnel bearing down on us. I trod water while we decided what to do next. Fortunately, Amana was a powerful swimmer.

'We either go back to the castle ruins and try to find some other way out, or we swim under here and hope the tunnel slopes up on the other side. Sometimes cunning old craftsmen deliberately blocked passages with water to discourage possible pursuers.'

'If we go back, Teryn and the others may have broken through with axes and ropes to rescue us, Lord.'

'I wonder if Nyrblos can hear us down here. He can't be far away, surely.' Why hadn't I thought of him before? I felt carefully for the disc in the leather wallet on my belt. Amana had hers tightly between her hands. We both concentrated hard on Nyrblos. Nothing happened.

'He can't hear us,' I said, 'we must be too far under the marshes.'

'Wait, Lord,' she gasped, '*something* is calling me. It isn't Nyrblos, but it's using his communicator.' I steadied her in the water to help her concentration. 'It's calling us forward, Lord.'

'Can we trust it?'

'I'm sure we can.'

'Right, then, forward it is.' We replaced the communication discs carefully, filled our lungs with air, and struck out together under the dark water. I counted the strokes as I swam, intending to save enough air and energy to turn and swim back if I did not find an airspace below the roof before the twentieth stroke. It was my right arm and my legs that were supplying most of the motive power: my left hand clung firmly to the leather belt of Amana's tunic. At the eighteenth stroke my head broke the surface. We paused and gasped gratefully at the cool, damp air, fresher here than on the castle side of the water barrier.

'Your voice was right. I wonder who it was.'

'Could Zotala guide us from so far away?' she asked.

'I don't think so, though his power is great. Did it sound like the voice of a man?'

'Not really, Lord; it was more of a *thought* than a voice.'

From the point we had reached, the tunnel climbed slowly upwards again, and the water grew correspondingly shallower as we walked. There was a definite current discernible in the air: the signs were good. Gradually, the blackness began to disperse. It was still very gloomy, but from some unknown source ahead of us there was a faint silver light. A few metres more and I could see Amana in the twilight. The swimming had removed most of the mud and she looked as lovely as ever despite our ordeal.

The light grew brighter with every step until we stood on the threshold of a small room at the side of the main tunnel. Here, resting securely in a simple wooden cradle, lay a crystal sphere about a metre in diameter. As we entered the room, the light faded almost to nothing: a glow so faint, it would not have been discernible beyond the walls of the room.

'Greetings, Black Lion and Queen Amana,' said a voice inside my head. I looked at her and knew that she had heard it too.

'The Life Sphere of Kalun!' I whispered.

'That is one of the names by which I am known; more accurately I am a co-ordinator sphere.' Conducting a conversation with a telepathic voice inside my head was disconcertingly like talking to myself.

'May I ask how you got here?' I asked.

'Zotala was only partly right,' said the voice of the Sphere. 'When the Wizards attacked Kalun forty years ago and Zotala and his forces were temporarily overwhelmed, a small group of priests escaped with me, intending to hide me in the labyrinth below the Rain Mountains. Unfortunately they were destroyed by a wer-beast who had travelled to Kalun with the Wizards' armies. This wer-beast like most of his kind was old and cunning. He had joined the expedition not because he wished to serve Andros but to see what gain there might be for himself. This was the great weakness in the Wizards' forces: neither trusted the other, and their allies were concerned only with personal gain, motivated by a mixture of greed and fear of their masters. The wer-beast, powerful in its own right, had no particular fear of Andros. It had been living in an ancient fortress at the edge of the swamp even before Andros rose to power in Abarak.' There was a brief pause in the flow of information from the Life Sphere, as though it was allowing time for us to digest what it had said so far.

'Zotala was mistaken in thinking his priests had taken their own lives?' I asked.

'That is so,' agreed the Sphere. 'The bodies had lain undiscovered in the labyrinth for a long time. It was almost impossible to tell what had happened. As I have said the

wer-beast was cunning: it had arranged the corpses peace-
fully and removed all signs of the struggle. It hoped in this
way to confuse whoever found them – Zotala or the Wizards.'

'Did it know what you were?' I asked.

'Not completely. I have certain built-in safeguards: I am
totally benign to all life forms; I cannot lie, but I can
withhold information from those who do not know the codes
of Zotala. Also I have the protection of a very potent force
field. I tried to persuade the wer-beast to return me to Kalun,
but by now Zotala had counter-attacked and the Wizards'
armies were all around the city. The beast decided to return
with me to its lair below the swamps. I calculated the chances
of being discovered here by one of Andros's creatures, but
they were slight. The greatest possibility of discovery was
during the journey but the wer-beast had human form by
day and concealed me in a peasant's cart load of peat which
he drove slowly along the bank of the Taran. It was not easy
to work out my precise location because the peat effectively
blocked my sensors, but I was able to read the wer-beast's
mind and use his senses to some extent as we journeyed.'

I raised an eyebrow interrogatively.

'I can enter minds to communicate with them and read
their answers,' explained the Sphere, 'but I have no control
over them. My powers are strictly limited to offering advice
and persuading by presentation of what I believe to be facts
and logical arguments.'

'*Believe* to be facts?' asked Amana.

'There are no certainties,' answered the Sphere, 'all data
is suspect. I cannot even prove my own existence, but my
calculations tell me that it is very likely, so I believe it to be
a fact and use it as a premise for other deductions.'

'How did the wer-beast reach this chamber?' I asked.

'There are three possible entrances, at least,' said the
Sphere. 'You were caught by an ancient trap in the castle
dungeons, put there by the wer-beast's ancestors, who built
the castle. The purpose was to drown or entomb raiders who
penetrated the outer defences. The garrison, holding the
mechanism shut, descended into this chamber using a

portable ladder which they carried here with them. Control wires in this wall,' it indicated them with a ray of light like a pointing finger, 'can be used to unlock and re-set the trap. In case raiders pass the water barrier through which you swam, there are two exits leading from here to the marshes. Normally the wer-beast uses these instead of the passage from the castle, but it is some time since he has been here. He is cunning, but not intelligent, and his memory is imperfect. He still does not fully realise what I am, and when he does think of me he has difficulty in deciding whether to try to trade with Andros or Zotala. Although I am not allowed to control his mind, I can divert it, so when he begins thinking of disposing of me to Andros I fill his head with thoughts of food and drink, of hunting and capturing prey, until I am forgotten again.'

'Can you guide us to the exits, if I carry you?'

'I can, but there is a risk that Andros's creatures will see us before you can rejoin the army.'

'I'll stay and guard the Sphere while you fetch reinforcements,' volunteered Amana.

'This is said to be the most precious thing in Derl Wothor, but to me you are far more precious. I will not be separated from you, even for the sake of the Sphere. We go together.' I hoisted the crystal globe out of the simple wooden cradle made for it by the wer-beast and held it in front of me. My hands did not quite touch the softly glowing crystal because the force-field insulated it from me. It felt as though I was carrying a weight suspended from a powerful magnet. The Sphere generated just enough light to illuminate the passage ahead of us.

'My sensors should give ample warning of an enemy in the tunnel,' said the Sphere, 'but I cannot yet detect life-forms in the marsh above, if there are any.' Despite its size, the Sphere was not as heavy as I had expected it to be, but it was awkward and cumbersome. If danger threatened I would not be able to draw my sword very quickly.

'Amana, just in case of sudden attack, draw my sword and carry it ready to hand to me.' She withdrew the heavy

Darian steel and carried it ready as we moved on through the tunnel.

'Look at the wall, where the beam shines,' said the Sphere. There was nothing that I could discern except a small stone projecting slightly from the wall of the passage.

'Press it,' suggested the Sphere. Amana pushed the stone carefully. 'Harder,' said the globe, 'it was intended for the heavy claws of a wer-beast.' She pressed as hard as she could and the projecting stone vanished into the wall. A section of stone slid back to reveal a doorway and a flight of stairs. They were barely wide enough to accommodate the Sphere with my arms around it, but with only centimetres to spare I struggled through. The stairs rose steeply until my head brushed against the damp lower branches of a clump of bushes which masked the secret exit. Amana wriggled past me and peered carefully in all directions.

'All clear, Lord, as far as I can see.'

'My sensors do not detect anything hostile,' confirmed the Sphere. I forced my way through the bushes and out on to the swampy surface of the marshes of Abarak. For the first time in forty years the Sphere was out on the surface of Derl Wothor, but it was not the place I would have chosen for its reappearance: we were not far from the heart of Andros's dark kingdom; his creatures lurked in the swamps around us, and the sun had set.

Enough of a glow remained in the eastern sky for me to tell which way to travel, but only by craning my neck to the side of the Sphere could I see where I was going. Some of the most serious and dramatic moments in life – on Derl Wothor as well as on Earth – are perilously close to comedy. As I struggled through foul-smelling swampland that was often knee-deep, holding the co-ordinator globe in my arms, I felt for all the world like a demented allotment holder carrying his prize pumpkin to the horticultural show. I laughed.

'Lord?'

'Nothing wrong, my love, I'm laughing.'

'Lord?' she sounded puzzled.

'This globe is the most important and valuable object in

Derl Wothor. The security of millions of people depends upon its reaching Kalun safely. It should be inside a steel cage on a war waggon drawn by black stallions and guarded by a thousand hand-picked warriors. It should have heralds and outriders with banners. Zotala should be riding ahead of it, the Tiger on its left and I on its right in full ceremonial armour. There should be bright sunshine, blue sky, white doves flying and my beautiful queen in a jewelled tunic riding beside me in the place of honour.' I laughed until the Sphere rocked in my arms. 'And the reality is a tired, half-drowned man and woman squelching through the swamp, peering behind every dark bush for fear of ambush.' My arms were aching and I hoisted the Sphere above my head like a Zulu warrior carrying away the spoils of war.

'I think I can see the ruin, Lord,' said Amana excitedly.

'Good. I'll be glad to hand this over to Teryn for safe keeping while I have a bath and a meal. I don't know which I want most: rest or food.'

'Can I try to carry it a little way?' she asked.

'No, my love, there's strength as well as love in your heart, I know truly, but if I once put it down I doubt if I could raise it again without a long rest, and every second we spend in this foul marsh is an invitation to Andros.'

We slogged on towards the castle ruin; our camp lay just across the river from it. As we approached we heard the faint sounds of spades on stone growing louder. The voice of Teryn could be heard in the distance shouting encouragement.

'Harder, lads! We *must* break through. Keep digging.'

Red eyes were watching us from behind the swamp bushes. Two became four, a dozen, a score; they were trying to surround us. I set the Sphere down and took my sword from Amana. She drew her own and we stood back to back with the globe between us. There were a hundred red eyes around us now, and they were closing in fast.

'Teryn,' I roared, in the direction of the castle. 'Teryn, bring men quickly. The wer-beasts are attacking.' The digging noises stopped. Loud and clear across the darkness, Teryn shouted.

'Where are you, Lord?'

'Over here, south of the ruin. Hurry!' Then I had no more time to shout. There were snarling, biting, clawing *things* rushing in from every side. Half-men, half-beast, they incorporated the worst of both. I was more tired than I had realised, although Amana must have guessed when she offered to try to take the Sphere. My timing was off and there was only a fraction of my usual strength in the sword strokes. Three wer-beasts wallowed in blood at my feet, but they were not dead. They continued to howl and writhe horribly. Amana had a sword in one hand, her silver dagger in the other. She was doing the wer-wolves more damage than I was at the beginning; but instead of draining away as I fought, my strength was slowly returning.

The creatures were trying to insinuate themselves between Amana and me. The Sphere was big, and that made a gap between us. Two or three were already snarling and clawing at her back as they scrambled over the Sphere to reach her. One had her long black hair in its mouth and was trying to pull her down.

A great stroke of steel and I beheaded it. I thrust the Sphere aside. 'Light!' I ordered, and dazzling white radiance sprang from it into the eyes of the wer-wolves. For a second they howled and leapt back startled by the glare. In that second I seized the jaws of the brute that was savaging her sword arm, tore them apart with a sound like ripping canvas and hurled the dying beast three metres into the air. The tiredness had gone. In its place was the same terrible anger which had surged through me when I fought the giant. I was roaring in a language that Amana did not know. This was not the strange language Mark Sable had used on distant Earth; this was not the ancient speech of Dar, spoken when the first Black Lion had reigned in Daris. These were war cries of Zotala's original space guards: professional fighters, trained killers from a savage dangerous world, part of an unimaginably distant galaxy.

'*Vashka, vashka, vashka! Niho zilan!*' Over and over, louder and louder, I could hear myself shouting and the sword sang with me, slicing flesh and breaking bone. I became aware slowly that the red eyes were all gone. Dimly I recognised Teryn and a great mass of Darian soldiers with him. Slowly, like a man in a trance, I lowered the sword. The battle fury left me.

'Help me, Teryn,' I said softly, 'I'm tired.' He guided the sword into its sheath, ordered men to pick up the Sphere, and led me back towards the Taran and the boats. There was awe in his voice when he spoke.

'Lord, you and the Queen slew most of the beasts before we could reach you. Never have I seen such strength and anger.' He pointed to the carnage. 'Lord, their bodies are scattered like leaves across the marshes.'

'Teryn, are they dead? They did not seem to die when I first struck them, but then the fury of the Old World came upon me.'

'Lord, some still live, but they are hacked and maimed; others are torn, as though rent by the hands of giants. A few are truly dead.'

'The truly dead were slain by Amana's silver knife. She did well to remember the words of the wiseman of Kalaford.'

'What strange words were you shouting, Lord? I thought at first it was the language of the beasts.'

'It was the language of beasts, the beasts from which I am descended,' I answered. 'Teryn, I came, or rather, the first Lion, whose reincarnated spirit I bear, came to Derl Wothor millennia ago. He came from a savage, dying world, part of a distant galaxy. He knew little then, save how to guard his friends and kill his enemies. He knew how to hate and how to destroy. It was not much of a talent, but it served him well in those long forgotten times. There was a war cry from his distant home world which he never forgot.' I paused.

'*Vashka* means "kill". *Niho zilan* means "let none remain alive".' I sighed and looked at Amana. She understood. She *knew*. Her hand gripped mine tightly. 'Teryn,' I went on, 'as centuries passed, the essence of the Lion learned more of

94

love and gentleness, but the primeval fury and hatred are still there, indelible in my soul. Faced with the bestial savagery of the wer-creatures, I destroyed them because my anger was more terrible than theirs. *I did not win because I am a man, but because I am an older and more terrible beast.*'

We reached the bank of the Taran and loaded the Sphere into the boat. Six Darian soldiers travelled with it, and the other boats formed an escort around it. I wondered whether Andros knew that it was so close to his stronghold. If he did, what action would he take to capture it? I peered down into the dark waters of the Taran. Did Andros's creatures lurk in the unseen depths? Nothing moved. Nothing but the oars disturbed the river.

The Sphere, glowing softly, was lifted out and taken to a tent in the centre of our camp. I called a meeting of my captains.

'The Sphere has been found. Half our task is completed, but we must keep moving south, raiding as we go, until we have news of the Tiger. Teryn, take 200 men and escort the Sphere to Kalun. Greet the Lord Zotala in my name and tell him that I am continuing south as planned. As soon as you have delivered the Sphere, come south and rejoin me. I shall need every man, when we storm the pirates' lair. Soldiers of Dar, I thank you all for the part you have played in recovering the Life Sphere.'

Teryn marched north at first light with his 200 powerful warriors. I watched his troop moving away towards Kalun before I gave orders for the main force to head south with me.

Chapter Eleven

The Pirates of Barak

Day followed uneventful day as we headed south through the bleak empty lands west of the Taran. From time to time a raid resulted in the capture of a swamp dweller or two, but none knew of the Golden Tiger. Five days after the Sphere had gone north with Teryn, my forces arrived at the point where the river emptied itself slowly and reluctantly into Taran Reach. This was really a large tidal estuary leading to the Sound of Qua and the Forbidden Islands beyond. The Reach was heavily silted up and the sluggish river found its way into the estuary only with difficulty.

If the legends were true, and if what we had gleaned from our handful of captives was reliable, the secret Citadel of Andros now lay a few miles to the north-east: buried in plague-ridden swamp-jungle, inhabited by cannibals, head-hunters and primitive atavistic sub-men. My Darians feared nothing, but I did not wish to take them through that fever saturated territory. If there had been any indication that the Golden Tiger was a captive in Andros's castle, then we would certainly have laid siege to it.

Perhaps it was some kind of deep, telepathic bond between the Tiger and me; perhaps it was ancient wisdom from Zotala and the Life Sphere; perhaps it was the even more ancient wisdom of Nyrblos – *something* was prompting me to concentrate on reaching Barak, rather than striking directly at Andros through the swamp. I wondered from time to time if some strategic, military caution deterred me from assaulting the swamp wizard's citadel. It was a strong Darian force that I led, but Andros was no mortal foe. An army attacking his stronghold would need Zotala's skills as well as the Lion and Tiger at its head. I felt that a successful raid on the hidden citadel of Andros lay a long way in the future – perhaps two or three incarnations ahead. I also felt an undeniable urge to go to Barak. Something or someone there was calling me, and I could not get the pirate city out of mind until the call had been answered. What worried me most was whether the call was from friend or foe. Andros must know of our presence by this time – an irritant upon his western flank. Was the hunch I felt about Barak anything to do with Andros's dark magic? I also had a deep sense of foreboding whenever I thought about the pirate city. I remembered the words of Zotala, of Conos the Blind Seer, and of Nyrblos. Was it in, or near, Barak that this dark destiny waited?

I pushed the strange forebodings to the back of my mind and crossed the silted estuary to study its eastern bank. What I saw I did not like. There was no real beach or coastal margin as such. The swamp jungle met the treacherous salt mud of the estuary. Every tree offered concealment to an ambush, and men were at a disadvantage fighting in mud against swamp creatures with flippers or webbed feet. I returned from the eastern bank and looked westwards. Just across the empty lands through which we had marched lay the forest, separating us from the friendly fields and villages of my South Feudatory.

'Lord,' said Amana softly, 'could we not make rafts and sail to Barak?' Certainly the timber was there, and, although rafts were ungainly and difficult to handle, the Reach was comparatively calm and sheltered. Only on rounding Barak Head in the Sound of Qua would we be in danger of encountering rough water. The more I thought about Amana's idea, the more it appealed to me.

Most of the expert woodsmen were in Teryn's 200 guarding the Sphere on its journey to Kalun, but there were enough sturdy axemen left with me to make short work of the trees we needed. Darian muscle hauled the logs to the water's edge, and Darian skill roped them together. Three layers deep we lashed them, with each layer at right-angles to the one below it. We cut long poles for each raft because the Reach was shallow and many wide sand banks lay below its placid surface.

My captains allocated a dozen men to each raft, and one by one we launched the cumbersome floats into the Reach. In the foremost raft, I pushed experimentally at the muddy bed of the estuary and felt the heavy logs responding to the effort. We tried to keep as close as possible to the eastern shore, but the sand banks often forced us out into deeper waters, where the poles exercised less control. The tide was running with us and combined with the slowly flowing river current to move the rafts at a fair pace.

The estuary widened, and, as the sun rose, vapour came up off the water, almost totally obscuring the heavily wooded western shore. A few miles more and that western shore was only a vague dark line, something to be guessed at through the mist.

As the day wore on and the mist shrouded sun sank slowly behind the western horizon, I began looking for safe moorings for the night. It was hard to estimate how far we had travelled, but we were doing better than marching speed and with much less effort. We had been sailing for ten or eleven hours, so we had covered forty or fifty miles. That meant we were roughly half way between the point where the river joined the estuary and Barak Head. As long as we kept close to the eastern shore we ought not to be in any real danger from the Sound or the open sea beyond.

I was already thinking ahead to the attack on Barak. In fairness to the corsairs I intended to ask first for free passage across their bridges over the Abarak River. They might refuse point blank, or they might agree and then attack treacherously as we crossed. There were more than enough of us to surround Barak; the problem was to reach it by crossing the river separating the swamp jungles of Andros from the desert of Kelnos. To cross Barak Bay on rafts would be suicide; the corsairs' swift ships would run us down. The answer seemed to be to sail to the eastern tip of Barak Head, beach the rafts and use the jungle edge for cover for the last fifty miles. Rounding the headland and sailing north to Barak would be much easier, but even if we hugged the eastern shore we would still be vulnerable to the corsairs' fast galleys and the heavy bronze rams on their bows.

We found a safe mooring and posted guards on the seaward and landward sides of the rafts. The night passed uneventfully despite the occasional stirrings from the swamp jungle and the baleful glow of predatory eyes that saw our strength and looked elsewhere for food. We ate a quick dry breakfast at first light and pushed the rafts downstream again. Once more tide and current were running with us, and we made good speed down the Reach, as the sun rose slowly higher. The mist was not as heavy as it had been during the previous day, and visibility was about fifty metres.

I pushed out into the channel to avoid what looked like a smooth grey sand bank some ten metres across. The raft behind was closer to the shore than mine, and the soldiers thrust their poles hard into the smooth grey surface to change direction. Their raft jolted into the obstruction and they pushed harder still to free it. There was a sudden flurry under the water, a miniature submarine earthquake. The sand bank rose into the air on legs like huge stone pillars, flinging both rafts over. I reached desperately for Amana and failed to find her. The raft struck me and drove me into the muddy water. It seemed an age before my breath returned. I coughed mud and water from my mouth and looked again for Amana. The river had become a mist shrouded hell of flying rafts and screaming, cursing soldiers.

The *thing* was about five metres high and twenty from nose to tail. It had a huge, ugly head, flattened and snake-like. The neck was slender compared to the great pear-shaped body. In addition to the pillar-like limbs there was a sort of living collar or frill below the jaws. These writhing tentacles, each two or three metres long, seemed to be there for passing food up to the mouth, which was open and roaring like thunder.

Among the shattered rafts and struggling soldiers I looked desperately for Amana, but there was no sign of her anywhere. I swam beneath the nearest rafts, which had overturned, but there was no sign of her. I fished out a young soldier and left him recovering on the bank, but he had not seen her.

'Find the Queen!' I ordered as the beast turned towards me. The baleful eyes glared horribly. The gigantic mouth opened and shut threateningly, revealing rows of sinister teeth. A great, grey tongue drooled over the lower jaw. The head bent towards me and the thunderous roar grew louder. I drew my sword and slashed murderously at the long, lolling tongue. The steel bit deeply into the grey flesh, and dark blood gushed down into the water. The roaring reached an insane crescendo and the jaws snapped close to my shoulder. Remembering Iban's words when we had fought the Jalnar, I struck at the nearest of the baleful eyes. It burst as the sword sank home and more dark blood welled up. Then tentacles like waggon ropes whipped furiously around me. The beast glared down with its one remaining eye and made for the deep water in the centre of the estuary.

As I struggled to tear the tentacles away I had a momentary glimpse of soldiers wading towards the beast swinging axes and swords, but it lashed its enormous tail and scattered them across the mud. I fought furiously to keep out of the jaws, and concentrated on freeing my sword arm first. Inch by inch I wriggled clear of the tentacles as we moved into deeper water. I realised the beast was swimming now and I knew it would submerge at any second. I drew a deep breath and pulled my sword arm clear just as it dived. I cut savagely at the tentacles that were pushing me closer to the jaws all the time. One by one they parted under the impact of the heavy Darian steel.

I felt no tiredness, no pain, just an urgent desire to kill the beast and go back to find Amana. As fast as I cut one tentacle through, it wound another round me. Over and over we threshed in the dark, swirling waters of the estuary. After what seemed an age, the thing broke surface again. I gasped air desperately and continued to cut at the coiling grey flesh that encircled my body and legs. Now that I could see once more my left hand darted to the long Darian dagger at my belt. Before the beast could dive again I had the dagger out, now I was cutting with both hands at the remaining tentacles. We crashed under the water again. My lungs were bursting as I cut and slashed at the alien flesh. Then I was free and kicking madly for the surface. Air! By all the Gods of Kalun, air! Gulping and gasping, I turned to look for the beast. A great scaly claw reached for me, clutched me and pulled me once more towards the fatal teeth.

I jammed my sandals against the upper jaw and launched what I thought would probably be my last blow against the remaining eye. My sword served me well, and the strong, black steel of Dar bit home. The monster was totally blind. Up went the hideous head in a terrible roar of pain and anger. The tail threshed wildly. The scaly claw gripped tighter, but the thing did not dive. While it was still in a state of shock from the loss of its sight, I started hacking at the claw that held me. The scales were tough, but not impenetrable. The dagger and sword flaked them away relentlessly. I began cutting into the claw itself. There was a renewed roar from the beast, and, with a sudden reflex action, the claw jerked open. I fell into the water, went down, broke surface again and saw the jaws groping for me. I stabbed up at the roof of the open mouth and the head jerked violently away from the pain of the blade. The teeth clashed loudly as the jaws closed, searching for me again in the blackness.

In the distance I heard shouts and the clash of steel on steel, but I could see nothing through the mist, and the beast was still demanding my attention. The fight seemed to have lasted an aeon, and all I wanted was to get back to search for Amana. The beast must die, and quickly. The battle fury of the Old World surged through me. It was this beast's sudden eruption which had taken her from me. I *hated* the beast. Now I was on the attack. This time I was the predator. I drove the dagger up to the hilt in the disproportionately slender neck and hung on like a mountaineer hanging on to his ice axe in a blizzard. The neck swung up taking me with it. I locked both arms around it, then swung my legs up as well and locked them in a scissor grip that nothing but death would break. My arms were free to fight.

The neck turned, writhed and twisted in every direction, but I clung like a limpet, and, as I clung, I cut. The short blade stabbed and the long blade sliced. Dark blood jetted from severed arteries. The movements grew slower. The huge legs stirred the water feebly. The wounded neck drooped. The head dipped below the surface. The huge carcase rolled slowly on to its side, and I flung myself clear.

I was completely disorientated, and for a minute or two I did not know which way to swim. Then I got my bearings from the position of the misty sun and the direction of the current. I reached the bank and resumed my search for Amana. A few moments later I found a soldier floating semi-conscious with an arrow in his shoulder. I carried him to the bank, removed the shaft and staunched the flow of blood. He opened his eyes and whispered, 'Pirates, Lord, out of the mist . . . Three or four galleys . . . ' He gritted his teeth with pain. 'They took . . . the Queen . . . ' He lost consciousness for a moment. 'I'm sorry, Lord, we tried . . . ' Again he broke off, gasping with pain.

'Was she still alive when you last saw her?'

'Yes, Lord, alive and fighting them.'

'Praise the White Gods!'

'Lord, we took one ship before they escaped, perhaps two; then I was hit and fell into the water.'

I left him propped against the bank and ploughed heavily through the mud, shouting as I ran. Two captains hurried towards me: Uxal of Janda and Varon of Casada. Uxal was about thirty years old, tall, brown-haired, bronzed and bearded. He came of an aristocratic family, a merchant adventurer who would have carried the flag of Dar to hell and back again. Varon was short, but broad as a door, and immensely strong. Casada was a small town on the Aval, the boundary between Dar and Valdar. Technically, Varon was one of my allies rather than a Darian citizen, but neither country ever noticed the difference. His father was the miller at Casada and when he was not soldiering young Varon was a prize fighter.

'Lord, we thought the beast had killed you,' said Uxal, 'before we could follow it, the corsairs attacked us.'

'I know. There's a young Darian back there with a pirate's arrow wound in his shoulder. He'll live, but he needs help. Send someone.' Uxal's troop were close behind him. He gave a swift order and two Jandans went to find the wounded man.

'What happened, Lord?' asked Varon.

'No time for the full story. I slew the beast and swam back.' An icy fear more terrible than the beast's claw gripped my heart. Amana was in the hands of the corsairs.

'How many ships attacked us?'

'Four, Lord, as far as we could tell in the mist. They did not realise how many we were at first. They must have seen men struggling in the water after the beast awoke and assumed we were only a few score. When raft after raft appeared they broke off the fight and headed south,' said Varon.

'They've gone to warn Barak, Lord,' suggested Uxal.

'If they were attracted by the idea of captives to be taken easily from the water, they were probably slavers, Lord, heading for Three Towers Bay,' said Varon.

'Slavers often raid Taran Reach,' agreed Uxal. 'They strike inland at the primitive tribes in the southern marshes. The wildmen fetch good prices in Argath. In the circuses of Kiphol they fight to the death with dogs and bears . . . Their women are sent to the torture houses of Ramos . . . '

'Lord, we captured one galley before they broke off the fight,' said Varon.

'Bring it to me, quickly.'

'Yes, Lord.'

Already a plan was forming in my mind. The pirates could not have got that far ahead, but where were they going – Barak or Three Towers Bay? The captured galley appeared through the mist. The corsairs were all dead. The soldiers of Dar had not taken kindly to a surprise attack from pirates after their encounter with the monster. The slaves were still being unchained from their oars. One or two were Darian sailors, captured by corsairs over the last two or three years. Several were wild men from the swamps – these we released. Others were nomads from the Great Desert, who asked if they could travel with us to the mouth of the Abarak. While my captains were freeing and sorting the slaves, I was selecting 100 strong Darians to man the galley. She would have taken more, but I wanted to travel light and fast. Some of my 100 I chose for their seamanship, others for their enormous strength and size. I also took outstanding bowmen, swordsmen and axemen, javelin throwers and close combat men, whose long daggers were well notched with old victories.

In less than an hour I was ready to pursue the pirate galleys. Varon came with me, but I left Uxal in charge of the army, with orders to come to Barak as swiftly as the rafts would allow. I delegated to him whether to go on foot from Barak Head or whether to sail the rafts up the western side of the bay. If I overtook the galleys I would rescue Amana or avenge her death – and rejoin Uxal's rafts before the attack on Barak. If I did not overtake them, I would raid Barak itself with my 100 men and storm the prison where the slaves were kept. Uxal would then be able to move in while the pirates' attention was on me.

It was a wild, desperate plan, but I was already sinking into that black despair which the wise men had foretold. Slowly it was coming home to me that Amana might be dead already, that she might be killed aboard the pirate ship, that she might die in the slave prison at Barak, that she might be put to death unspeakably in the torture houses of Ramos, or one of the other cities of the League. If I went to Barak, she might be screaming her heart out in Ramos. If I attacked

Ramos, she might be dying in Barak.

Suddenly in the depth of my doubt and despair I remembered the disc Nyrblos had given me. I climbed to the top of the mast as though looking for the galleys we were pursuing, then I grasped the communicator tightly and concentrated on the strange, fronded figure of the tree-man.

'Nyrblos.' Alone at the mast-head I whispered his ancient name. 'Nyrblos, help me. Help us both.' The disc tingled a little. He was aware of me. I tried hard to empty my mind, to pick up his advice.

'Row.' Just that one word, but the tingling went on. 'Row. She lives.' The link was broken, but there was a tiny gleam of hope now in my deep mental and spiritual darkness. *She lives*. The words brought a new glow to the scattered ashes of my mind. I descended the mast as fast as a man could run and took the foremost oar from the rower. Varon sat opposite me. His deep chest and wide shoulders rippled with powerful muscles and sinews.

'In twenty minutes, Lord, I'll change the rowers. That way we'll make the best speed possible.' The voice of Nyrblos had been right. Rowing was the best thing for me. It was *action*. I would have gone insane at the mast-head staring through the mist for a glimpse of the corsairs. Like a huge, tireless automaton I pulled at the oar, over and over again. When it was time to change, I changed sides to bring a different group of muscles into action. Man after man rowed and rested. The Black Lion rowed on into the darkening mist where Taran Reach joined the Sound of Qua.

'Won't you try to sleep, Lord?' asked Varon, as he took his fifth turn opposite me.

'Not yet,' I panted grimly. 'If I stop rowing, I shall only begin to imagine what they're doing to Amana.' I felt like part of the great oar, dipping into the water and pulling against it; the wood had become an extension of my dulled mind. Exhaustion was the only anaesthetic available.

Chapter Twelve

The Prisoner of Barak

'Lord, it grows too dark to see.' Varon's voice reached me through the clouds of weariness gathering at the edges of consciousness.

'Is there a moon tonight?'

'Yes, Lord.'

'When?' I was still rowing as I spoke.

'Another hour, Lord.'

'We'll risk it. Hold her on course, Varon.'

'Lord,' he hesitated.

'Yes.'

'Lord, how will you fight if you are tired from the night's rowing?' His words penetrated my brain singly, like sling shots. It was several minutes before I grasped the significance of what he had said.

'You are a good friend, Varon, and you talk sense. At the next change I'll try to sleep. Double the forward lookouts and put extra men at the mast heads. We show no lights. If the corsairs have their lanterns lit this may be our chance to catch them.'

Varon gave a great sigh of relief. I rowed for another ten minutes, and then, at the change signal, staggered from the rowing bench to my cabin. One of Varon's men brought me a large flagon of sweet red Darian wine and I drank deeply before sinking on to the bunk. My mind was obsessed with thoughts of Amana. Where was she now? How many corsairs had raped her already? Had she fought free, leapt overboard and tried to swim for it? Was she drowned at the bottom of the sea, or chained at the bottom of the galley? Suppose I couldn't find her – suppose they took her to die in the torture houses of Kiphol. Few Darians knew the details of what happened in the hell dungeons of the League, but it was fact that Ramos, Kiphol and Argath created an insatiable demand for beautiful slave girls.

I fell at last into a troubled sleep, disturbed by strange dreams. Scenes tumbled over one another in a series of wild, kaleidoscopic nightmares. I was on top of the burning tower with Zotala hanging a blazing medallion round my neck. I plunged through grey spaces between the galaxies and landed in a prison exercise yard. Teryn climbed the wall, cutting down guards with his axe. I escaped into a cave of jalnars and scaly green giants. My sword broke, and I lost my dagger in the struggle. The cave floor turned to mud, and tentacles pulled me down into it. Pirates were dragging Amana away, and I could not run in the heavy slime. Every movement I made was slow and exaggerated. She broke free and leapt into deep, dark water. The mud still held me. A great beast swam after her. The mud dissolved and I caught hold of the beast's throat, pulling it like an oar, like an oar, like an oar . . . Now Amana was on an auction block in Ramos, her tunic torn away, her beautiful bronzed body exposed to the cruel eyes and callous hands of the buyers from the torture houses.

There was the sound of tearing wood, and I found myself suddenly awake, soaked with sweat and gripping the side of the bunk. Unable to sleep again, I climbed the mast once more and tried to contact Nyrblos. The disc began tingling. 'Do not lose hope; she still lives, but I cannot locate her exactly. There are strong vibrations near Barak and they have a close affinity with yours. I do not think you will find the corsairs at sea; I have no vision of it. Someone or something in Barak needs you.'

107

'Is it Amana?' I asked.

'I can't be sure. I hear the call, but I cannot identify the source.' The tingling died away and I felt helpless and isolated on the mast-head. Two look-outs nearby were straining their eyes into the moonlit night. The oars creaked and splashed rhythmically. The bronze ram at the bows cut purposefully through the water. No breath of wind stirred. It would have been pointless to try to use the sail. To get my mind off what might be happening to Amana, I tried to think of Uxal and the bulk of the army. Where were they? How far behind us were the cumbersome rafts? My thoughts went out to Teryn's 200. Where were they? Had they reached Kalun safely? Had Zotala taken charge of the Sphere? Was Teryn already heading for Barak? The questions buzzed in my head like a swarm of angry hornets. Each one stung my mind with sinister pictures of potential disaster: Teryn and his men wiped out by Andros's horrors below the Rain Mountains; my army annihilated by corsair war galleys and sea-monsters before it could reach Barak. My fault – it was all my fault – I felt I was making one hopelessly wrong decision after another. The depression and despair were getting to me again. If Amana died . . . if Andros captured the Sphere . . . if Uxal's rafts were wrecked . . . it would be *my fault*. Would it have been better if Zotala had not found me on distant Earth? I had to break this mood, it was destroying me . . .

Nyrblos said Amana lived. Teryn was as capable as any man of escorting the Sphere safely to Kalun: I could not have entrusted it to a better soldier. Uxal was a careful and experienced commander: the army was as safe with him as with me. Then the doubts came back. Who would destroy the monsters for them if I wasn't there? Deep down I knew that it was only the grief and shock at Amana's capture that was causing the guilt, depression and confusion; but knowing the cause was one thing and fighting it was another.

Slowly, far too slowly, the moon rose higher, sank and then set. The night edged away reluctantly. Dawn came up clear and bright. Here in Barak Bay the mists of Taran Reach did not form. Visibility was good. I looked in all directions, but there was no sign of the corsairs. I could not understand how we had failed to overtake them. All I could assume was that they had reached Barak harbour ahead of me. I decided to make all possible speed for the pirate city itself. Already the northern shore of Barak Bay was visible ahead of us, the ramparts surrounding the harbour and the strong-walled stone houses of the corsairs. Barak was an independent city state, and the pirates had many enemies. There were factions and rival groups within the city as well, from what I could recall. The corsairs' friendship was short-lived and unreliable; their enmity and suspicion endured. Their unity depended upon the seriousness of external threats and political pressures. It was in their fierce independence and lack of cohesion that our best hope lay.

'Slow down for the run in,' I ordered. If we made a normal approach it might be possible to enter the harbour itself without being challenged. I knew where the slave prisons were; in previous incarnations I had raided Barak before, but these memories were vague and general rather than exact. The prisons were extensive and deep: the more valuable slaves were kept in the lower dungeons to minimise their chances of escape. This was where I needed the kind of help Nyrblos might be able to give, if he could work at those depths.

As I watched the harbour growing closer I climbed the mast again and signalled to Nyrblos. The response was significantly stronger than it had been last time. Nyrblos was either closer than before, or he had found some way of improving our communications now that he was more familiar with my mind. His thoughts were sharp and clear as they reached me.

'I am receiving other signals as well as yours, but they are fainter,' said Nyrblos. I wondered whether Amana had lost her communicator. The pirates had probably taken it thinking it was a coin. 'If I amplify them and relay them to you, your communicator will vibrate more strongly as you approach their source.' Nyrblos had gone again, but at least I had something to work on.

We continued moving almost casually towards the harbour mouth. There were a score of pirate galleys at anchor, but none moved to stop us as we crossed the bar into the harbour itself. Varon stood with me in the bows as we rowed steadily across the fortified inner pool. If the vessels we had pursued were among those at anchor, they would surely have warned the rest of the corsairs that a huge Darian army was coming down Taran Reach on rafts. War galleys would have been out in Barak Bay to destroy the rafts before they could land. That was what I would have done, but was it what the pirates' commander would have done? There were several possibilities. Perhaps they were waiting for the rafts to get within range of their ballista and catapults before sending out galleys to intercept. Perhaps they were waiting for an attack from *rafts* and did not realise that my Darians had captured a galley. The third possibility was the least welcome: perhaps the galley carrying Amana had not been heading for Barak, but *Argath* or another League city.

The only way to know whether she was in the slave pens was to attack them and find out. We had reached an empty space on the mooring wall of the inner harbour, and I commended the seamanship of my Darians as they manoeuvred into it as though they tied up in Barak a hundred times a year. The slave quarters were about 300 metres to the left of us.

The wharf was deserted in the bright early morning sun. We left a skeleton crew on board in case of emergency while Varon and I led the rest of our men over the gang plank and on to the quay. Every eye was keenly on the look out for corsairs as we moved along the stone slabs above the water's edge. The first pirate I saw lay dead, or drunk, outside a tavern door. A stray dog eyed us curiously as he slunk among heaps of decaying garbage in the alley beside the tavern. There was no other sign of life at all.

The slave pens and prison buildings behind them were clearly visible as we rounded a curve in the harbour wall – and so were the guards. Slaves meant gold, and the corsairs lived and died for gold. A bar of bullion had neither the motive nor the legs to escape – slaves had, and the slave pens were secured accordingly.

I was gripping my sword in one hand and Nyrblos's communicator in the other. The metal disc began to vibrate noticeably, and in the same instant the guards saw us coming. They were talking excitedly together and pointing in our direction. We kept walking steadily, as though it was the most natural thing in Derl Wothor for ninety Darians to stroll along the waterfront of Barak. As we walked my bowmen surreptitiously selected their targets; my javelin throwers calculated distances. We were fifty metres from the pens before we were challenged. A swarthy corsair in a green tunic stepped out from among the dozen outer guards and pointed his crossbow at me. He shouted something I couldn't hear distinctly at that distance, and I saw his grip on the bow tightening ominously. Without slackening pace two Darian bowmen fired from the left and right of me simultaneously. The pirate's finger must have been on the trigger when both black shafts transfixed him. The body toppled backwards; the crossbow bolt flew harmlessly into the air above him; red seeped across the green. The fight was on.

Arrows and javelins disposed of the remaining outer guards, while my swordsmen and axemen charged the gates of the outer pen. Stout steel splintered the wood around the bars and bolts. Varon's great muscles bulged as he heaved at the left hand gate. The disc in my hand increased its vibration as I threw my weight beside his. The gate creaked and gave a little, but something was still holding it. More Darians joined us. More axe blows fell on the weakening timber. There was a tearing crash as the gate burst inwards. Corsair guards had been trying to hold it against us; several of them were now pinned under it. We trampled them as we ran through. Varon paused long enough to despatch the survivors.

'I don't like a wounded enemy behind me, Lord,' he said simply.

The pens themselves were a confusing maze of small cells

111

and cages with narrow passages between.

'Amana!' My shout penetrated the noise of the fighting. I turned to Varon.

'Free the slaves. Arm them with the guards' weapons and turn them loose. They can help us, or cut their own way out of Barak. Either way they'll take the corsairs' attention.'

Axes smashed more doors, and slaves began pouring out into the narrow prison corridors, adding to the noise and confusion. The disc was almost tugging me forward by the hand, leading me down into the lower levels of the prison. Every few steps I paused and called her name, but there was no answering cry.

At the foot of the stairs leading to the third level I found a fat, bald, scar-faced guard with a gold ring through his nose. He looked so incongruous that I almost laughed aloud. He dropped his sword and raised his podgy hands pitifully.

'Do you speak Darian?'

'A little.'

'Good. Is there a girl in the prison? Light brown skin, long black hair, very beautiful, brought in a few hours ago?'

'All the women are on the lower level.' He pointed to the head of the next descending flight.

'Is that the deepest?'

'No, there's one below it for special prisoners.'

The disc was vibrating even harder, almost escaping from my fingers, pulling me towards the stairhead. I had no real wish to kill the fat pirate, but I had no intention of leaving him active behind me.

'Can you unlock this door?' I pointed to the nearest cell.

'Yes.' He indicated a bunch of keys on his belt.

'Open it and get inside.' He did so, trembling. I locked him in and threw the key ring to Varon.

'Free any slaves on this level, then bring a few men and follow me down. There are only two more levels.' I ran down the dark stairs. The primitive torches cast weird, flickering shadows as I brushed past them. Varon and my Darians were not far behind me. The confused sounds of freed slaves and fighting corsairs grew fainter above me as I ran on down

112

the stairs. They ended in a wide chamber with cell doors all around its walls. Unlike the higher level, this was formidably guarded. There were a score of vicious-looking young corsairs scattered around the room and almost as soon as I burst in among them I was at the centre of a ring of steel. There was no space to fight with finesse. I swung my sword in great scything arcs of death, too fast for the eye to follow, too powerful for a corsair's arm to parry. The madness of battle was intoxicating; it was a different level of awareness.

The ring widened, distorted and broke into fragments. It was no longer a confident, cohesive attack. A dozen separated survivors were trying desperately to stay alive. Killing the berserk murder machine which I had become was now a secondary objective. I ran the nearest man through and wondered for an instant as he fell if those wide glazed eyes had seen Amana a few hours earlier. His dying hand opened spasmodically. Had that hand struck her? Chained her? Locked the door of her cell? Another corsair went down, and another. Fists, blade, hilt and feet worked like the components of a death engine in top gear. In the background I heard Varon and the Darians near the door. The vibrating disc urged me towards the final stairway.

'Open the cells, Varon,' I called over my shoulder.

'Yes, Lord.'

These, the deepest stairs, were narrower and steeper than those I had already descended. The air was still, as though insulating the prisoners below from any movement or freedom of the upper world. The torches burnt dimly, casting a deep red glow over the dark stone of the walls. It was a more sombre and suffocating prison than those above – something designed to destroy the spirit.

The disc was like a living thing, urging and tugging in my hand. I followed its signals calling 'Amana' over and over again. The stairs ended in a domed vault cut straight from the rock. There were four cells around the base of the dome and three of their doors hung empty. Straight ahead lay one thick iron door, tightly locked and bolted. There was a small grating in the centre, but the light was too dim to reveal any of the cell's interior. I ran across the floor of the dome.

'Amana?'

I looked anxiously through the wide-barred grating. I could just make out a human figure lying on the floor of the cell. It stirred slightly as I called again.

'Amana?'

There was a soft footfall behind me and an explosive pain at the base of the skull. Fingers of red and black fog tried to strangle my consciousness. My knees sagged and I clutched the grating. Nyrblos's disc slipped to the rock floor. Instinctively I kicked backwards and made contact. Turning through the dizzying nausea I saw a hunchback, dressed in leather and holding a club. His deep set eyes glittered. His arms, long and powerful, hung down like the arms of an ape. He was spitting out blood and broken teeth, and mumbling curses. The club came down again, but this time I parried it with my sword. My vision was blurred, and my legs were still unsteady. I wasn't co-ordinating. Madly, incongruously I wanted to laugh. He looked like Punch. The club got under my guard. Those long, dangling arms were incredibly strong. The hunched, deformed shoulders were packed with muscle. I felt as though my ribs had been kicked by a horse. Winded, I doubled over in front of the door – momentarily helpless. Thoughts passed at lightning speed: would Varon be able to save Amana without me? It was ironic to die like this after everything that had happened, to beat trained swordsmen by the score and then lose to a cripple with a wooden club – even more ironic if Amana was on the other side of that iron door.

Through the mists of pain and nausea I heard a strange drumming, scrabbling sound and a choking gurgle. A foot caught the side of my face and I rolled sideways gasping in air again at last. My ribs felt as if they were alight, but I was *alive*. The club had *not* fallen. I staggered grimly to my feet and saw the explanation of the miracle. Two of the biggest arms I had ever seen, knotted with hard old muscle jutted out from the grating in the iron door. The hands at

the end of those arms had the hunchback by the throat, clear
of the ground. His eyes bulged; his face was purple. His feet
drummed on the iron door. He had dropped the club. His
hands clawed ineffectually at the huge arms that were lifting and strangling him. A javelin passed me from the foot of
the stairs, flying faster than a diving hawk. It transfixed the
hunchback's body, and the great hands released the corpse.

Varon stepped past me and retrieved his javelin. The huge
old arms withdrew and a craggy, brown face appeared.

'You took long enough to get here,' said a very deep
rumbling voice. I tried to roll the hunchback's body over to
find the key. The nausea returned. Varon finished cleaning
his javelin and came to help me.

'What's wrong, Lord?' he asked.

'The pirate clubbed him,' said the voice from the cell. 'It
would have killed a human being, but he always did have an
oaken skull, even when I was a boy.' There was a bellowing
laugh that made the iron door reverberate. 'Where's that
damned key?' Varon found it and unlocked the cell.

A grey-haired barrel supported by two tree trunks strode
out and stretched its arms luxuriously. 'I enjoyed that,' it
announced. A forefinger like a steel crossbow bolt prodded
Varon in the chest. 'You throw well, lad. I felt the door
shake.'

Varon smiled. Then bowed low. Suddenly, I realised who
the barrel was. Over forty years ago I had taught and
protected a young warrior, my ward until he came of age, my
King-Brother of the North, Zotala's other guard from the
beginning: this rugged old veteran was the Golden Tiger of
Valdar.

Chapter Thirteen

The Great Desert

The double impact of joy and disappointment jolted my mind like heavy blows across the skull, harder than the hunchback's club had struck. It was almost unbelievable that the Golden Tiger was alive, let alone still powerful and undaunted by experiences that would have destroyed most men.

He had been on the defensive for years against The League, against Andros, against Kelnos and their creations. He had withstood the hopelessness of the fruitless search for me, the anxiety when Zotala had left Derl Wothor, the repeated frustration of leading armies which were always too small.

He had been caught, somehow, somewhere in desert or swamp and brought here hostage. Perhaps corsair galleys had attacked a Valdarian ship while he was aboard. I had not yet had time to ask him. A gigantic hand dropped on to my shoulder like a poleaxe.

'Lion, you think too much and you don't drink enough.' The voice was gruff, but the old eyes were ecstatic. As we moved across the prison floor the hand on my shoulder conveyed the gratitude which he could never put into words. 'Tell me how you found me?' he asked.

'I was looking for a woman,' I said grimly. He started to laugh. 'You always were. It'll be the death of you . . .'

'It will, if I don't find her.' His laughter stopped as though cut with a sword. In the silence I remembered Nyrblos's disc and turned to pick it up.

'What's that?'

'It led me to you – it's some kind of long distance communicator. I had hoped it was leading me to her.' Just for an instant the old eyes clouded. 'Tiger, I was looking for you as well. You were our quest – hers and mine. She was helping me to find you. She's my Queen in Daris. Her name's Amana.'

'Daughter of Eldon of Kalaford?' he asked incredulously.

'You know her?'

'Known her since Eldon rocked her cradle. He's helped me in many a battle. How is he?'

'As great a warrior as ever.'

We were climbing the stairs to the upper levels when the Tiger's eye rested on a newly freed slave girl: a nomad from the southern desert, black haired, dark eyed, full breasted and sensuous. He swept her up over his shoulder with a swift, practised movement.

'If there's one thing I need more than a drink, it's a woman,' he explained simply. The girl did not struggle or scream. Despite his age, the Golden Tiger was magnetically attractive; she lay contentedly over his huge shoulder as he continued to climb. He stooped once more as we passed the body of a dead corsair, and helped himself to the pirate's sword. 'Too light,' he grumbled, 'but it'll do for now.' He looked at me. 'Tell me your adventures. How did you get back to Derl Wothor?'

'It'll have to wait a while.' I explained the present military situation quickly, and he nodded once or twice.

'Your hundred are more than enough. Remember the old times? We could cut our way out of here alone – just the two of us. How long before the rafts get here?'

'An hour, a day, two at the very worst.'

We reached the upper level. There were no live corsairs to be seen. Varon, big, calm and efficient, threw a ring of guards around the compound and began checking our original party

117

plus the freed slaves who'd joined us. We'd lost three dead, and five were wounded. The Tiger stooped over one of them and studied him closely. 'Past help and in great pain,' he said softly. His sword went in swiftly and mercifully. The moaning stopped, and the dead man's face relaxed. 'Let his spirit be born to a better future,' said the Tiger, looking north towards the Rain Mountains and wiping the sword slowly. He returned suddenly to the military problem.

'Uxal's men are coming from the east. They'll have to cross the mouth of the Abarak where the current is swift before they can reach the city. Or go a few miles north to the bridges. In those waters the corsairs could sink them all. We have to disable the galleys first,' he said.

'Agreed – and we have to hold the harbour wall.'

'Lord.' Varon had finished checking our forces and joined us.

'We have to destroy the ballista. Rafts cannot manoeuvre to avoid bombardment.'

'Three main objectives, and three of us,' said the Tiger. 'Any sign of a counter-attack yet?'

'Nothing yet, Lord,' called a guard on the perimeter.

'How many freed slaves?' I asked.

'Over a hundred with us, Lord,' answered Varon, 'and more than that loose in the city.'

'I'll take them and disable all the galleys I can find. I may try to . . . ' I broke off as a different idea occurred to me. 'We don't want to *disable* the galleys – we want to *use* them,' I shouted. 'We'll go out to *meet* Uxal – escort the rafts across the mouth of the Abarak.' It was obviously a better battle plan. Why had I not seen its advantages before? I looked across at the Tiger. He had one arm around the slave girl. His enormous right hand held a wine flagon. The girl was breaking bread for him and putting it to his lips between gulps of wine. He looked exactly what he was: a grand old warrior-king intent on living life to the full after months of deprivation. Between bread and wine he growled, 'I'll take fifty men and capture the ballista.'

'I'll guard the landing place, Lord,' said Varon, 'and do

what other damage I can. A few fires among their waterfront warehouses will keep them busy.'

Varon organised the groups quickly. The freed slaves were talking together excitedly. He raised a hand for silence and the talking died away. The eyes of the slaves were on us.

'You are free men and women again, but you have chosen to stay under my protection rather than try to escape alone . . . I need you now. Come with me to capture pirate galleys. We will free the rowers, and sail to meet my Darians who are already on their way to take this city. Once my army arrives your obligation ends: you can then choose weapons and supplies to journey home, or you can enlist as soldiers of Dar.' There were several anxious, bewildered faces, and I realised that almost half my group could not speak Darian. There was little time to find interpreters, but I called loudly for any who knew the desert languages and three came forward. They found a fourth who could make himself partly understood in the guttural growling speech used by the Wild Men of the swamps. They did their best to get the message across. I hoped that the remaining dozen who hadn't understood would have the sense to follow us and copy what the rest did.

The Tiger took his group off towards the steps leading up to the fortified ballista platforms. Varon's holding party spread along the quayside and took up defensive positions wherever cover presented itself. They would be hard to dislodge without a long bloody fight. The landing site was as secure as we could make it. I split my force into ten small raiding parties, leading the confused non-Darian speakers myself.

There were fourteen or fifteen galleys moored along our stretch of the harbour wall. The corsairs' fierce independence was our best ally that morning: there was no bureaucracy in Barak. A pirate served his own interests first, then those of his captain. Defence of their city and co-ordination of their urban resources were low on the pirates' list of priorities. In totalitarian Kiphol or Ramos, every ship entering or leaving harbour was logged by the Harbour Master and checked by his guards. The corsairs of Barak came and went as they pleased. A captain might know which vessels lay on either side of him, where they were from and where they were bound, but he would know it as waterfront gossip – not from the shipping records. Pirates were treasure hunters who kept their comings and goings secret.

We reached the nearest galley unchallenged. I indicated by signs that I wanted my men to jump aboard and attack any pirates they found. The only corsair on deck was staring up at the ballista platforms as I landed on the planks beside him. There were many ships to take, and I was not counting on much help from my heterogeneous polyglot boarding party. The corsair's head rolled across the deck and splashed into the water.

From the ballista platforms, high above us, came the sounds of grim hand to hand fighting. Shrieks and groans mingled with the heavy thuds of falling bodies. The clash of sword on sword and spear against shield rang loudly across the waterfront. It rang like an angry peal of ominous warning bells, and, at last, it roused Barak to its danger. Corsairs were appearing on galley decks and running out of waterfront alleyways. Like a horde of rats scrambling from holes in a derelict graveyard they scurried towards the ships. There was a dull roar of confused shouting: questions in different languages that no one stopped to answer; uncomprehended orders that few heard and fewer obeyed. The corsairs were a mob – a mindless, undisciplined rabble – as they milled about the quayside.

Flames began to lick upwards from two large warehouses. Varon's men were in action. The flames appeared again, farther north, running like the tide along the eastern bank of the Abarak. The crowds of Corsairs grew denser as more pirates emerged from fire-threatened buildings and made for the quay.

Like a thunderbolt thrown by an avenging god, the first huge ballista stone smashed into the middle of the seething crowd. The shouting rose to a roar of hysterical panic and fury. High on the ballista platform, his great bulk awe-inspiring even at that distance, stood the implacable Golden Tiger. Sweeping strokes of his sword conducted the stone fire, pointing out the areas where death was to fall next. The corsairs had tried to hold a tiger by the tail, I thought, but now that Tiger was free, and, by the Gods of Kalun, the pirates were paying heavily for their temerity. The waterfront was blazing, the quayside littered with crushed and dying victims of the stone guns, the hill below the ballista platforms strewn with the hacked corpses of the original ballista crews.

My freed slaves were doing considerably better than I'd thought they would. After a second's glance at the headless corpse at my feet they had dispersed over the galley in search of pirates. There were only a dozen corsairs in the cabins, and the ex-slaves were enjoying their revenge. I went down to the rowing benches and began snapping chains and pulling out shackles and staple-irons. Soon, despite the language problems, I had sixty followers instead of ten. The pirates' bodies were thrown contemptuously over the side, and I prepared to attack the next ship.

Alerted to their dangers now, the galleys were pulling away from the quayside. From those that were not moving, I deduced that we had captured six. Fierce fighting raged on three others where the boarding parties had met stiff opposition. The ship we were attacking was one that had just started to move. My sixty men swarmed savagely aboard her looking for corsairs. Those whom I had just freed from the rowing benches were gaunt, wild-eyed creatures, half-crazed with pain and hatred. I watched four of them drag down one pirate using only their bare hands. I heard him screaming as they tore him apart like animals, while I made for the helmsman.

He was a tall, wide-shouldered southerner, bigger and heavier than I was, and his knotted muscles showed the scars of several old sea battles. His eyes were a peculiar reddish-grey, like embers – he stared at me balefully before releasing the tiller and drawing an axe from his belt. My sword parried the axe, but it was a powerful stroke – and I had no intention of repeating the error I had made against the hunch-backed dwarf. He drew back his axe for another blow and I darted the sword point towards his throat. For all his size, the helmsman was fast. He jerked back as I stabbed and the point barely touched his skin. This time I was too far forward and slightly off balance as the axe came down. Instinctively I kept going forward, trying to get in under the blow. I took him around the waist and we crashed to the deck together. The axe-blade splintered the planks behind, only inches from my sandal. My hands and forearms moved up into a lethal grip around the helmsman's throat and closed there. He struggled wildly, trying to extricate his axe from the splintered planks. I crushed his throat until the struggling subsided, then with a final heave I forced the head sideways. His neck broke with a heavy crack, like a thick oak branch snapping. I scrambled up, retrieving my sword and turning to face whoever was behind. The giant southerner had given me a hard fight, and I was breathing heavily.

The deck behind was clear. My freed slaves had massacred the remaining corsairs, and were even now flinging the last of the bodies overboard. I lifted the dead helmsman and saw that the fire had gone out of his strangely coloured eyes. The body was only a sack of earth, soft and inert, but heavy and awkward. It sank like a stone beneath the dark waters of the Abarak. As the bubbles streamed up, I wondered where that man had sailed and fought, where he had built his powerful muscles, in which battles he had acquired his scars. What had those red-grey eyes seen across the wide oceans of Derl Wothor? Had he loved? Had he been loved? Or was he merely a crude, primitive barbarian, an intelligent beast, endowed only with the feelings of a beast? The bubbles failed to answer.

A ballista stone splashed into the water a cable's length ahead of the galley I had just captured. Instinctively I looked up towards the platforms. The Tiger was waving to attract my attention and pointing towards the far side of the estuary. I climbed the mast and looked where he pointed. Rafts! The army of Dar was in sight! I turned and looked again at the

Tiger. In a voice that carried clear up to the ballista platform I shouted. 'Sink the corsairs,' and pointed to the galleys that were moving.

Now that the pirates were at last realising their peril, they were reacting quickly and beginning to take effective action. They too had spotted the rafts and recognised the Army of Dar. They knew its reputation: as a fighting force on land, nothing could stand against it. The pirates' one hope lay in ramming the rafts before my men could land, or capture the bridges up stream. We already had a foothold, doggedly held by Varon's men. We commanded the inner harbour with the corsairs' own stone guns, and no power in Derl Wothor could dislodge the Golden Tiger from those craggy heights. They might starve him out, given time, but, even without the approaching rafts, the corsairs knew that Barak was seriously threatened. There was a desperate urgency about the way the six galleys we had failed to capture started towards Uxal's men across the strongly racing currents of the mouth of the Abarak.

I tore off a strip of sailcloth to use as a signal flag, and from the mast-head I transmitted a message to Uxal of Janda, commanding the rafts. From the nearest of the pirate galleys, pulling towards my raftsmen, a thin red shaft sped straight for me. It sang past my arm, pinning the sailcloth to the mast head. I snapped off the arrow, freed my makeshift flag and continued to signal. Another thin red shaft sped by, a metre away, and fell among the struggling mass of corsairs on the quayside. Someone on board that galley knew the secret military codes of Dar. Someone had read my signal to Uxal, and knew that if he received and obeyed that message the corsairs had no chance of destroying my Darians on the water. A third red shaft fell slightly short, embedding itself in the mast below me. I carried on signalling. At last I got the answer I was waiting for: 'Received and understood.' Uxal now knew that we had galleys too. I had ordered him to beach his rafts on the western bank, disembark and wait defensively until I could ferry our men over in the ships I had just captured.

As I was scrambling down the mast, a huge ballista stone scored a direct hit on the leading galley. It was a superb shot. The sail was ripped down, the mast leaned drunkenly and the massive projectile tore into the hull. Screams and cries of terror echoed over the water as the stricken galley began to sink. The other five redoubled their effort to get out of range. The next stone missed, but the one after that struck the stern of the fifth galley and dragged it below the water like an invisible hand. More panic stricken screams echoed across the water. The next few shots all fell short: the four surviving pirate vessels were out of effective ballista range.

On the far bank, the western bank, I could just make out the bronzed, bearded figure of Uxal supervising the beaching of the rafts and the disembarkation of our army. The corsair galleys were turning south, moving swiftly with the current and trying to attack the rafts still pulling in from Barak Head. These raftsmen farther down the convoy would not yet have received Uxal's order to land on that western bank and take up their defensive positions. They would be vulnerable to the heavily armoured ramming prows of the galleys. Even one galley could overturn forty or fifty of the clumsy rafts – four could drown half the Darian army. I climbed back to the mast-head and waved the 'ceasefire' signal to the Tiger, then, taking the helm myself, I pointed first to the moving corsair galleys and then to the rowing benches.

Four men to an oar, my ex-slaves crowded the benches, pulling harder as free men than they had ever pulled before. The bows began to lift over the wave crests as the galley sped forward into mid-stream. Within minutes we were overhauling the slowest of the four corsairs and I signalled for a boarding party. Armed to the teeth with weapons looted from the pirates they had massacred, and still thirsting for vengeance, newly freed slaves lined the starboard rail as we overtook our quarry. A quick movement of the tiller and our armoured prow sheared off half a dozen oars, temporarily crippling the corsairs. The vessels locked together momentarily, and in that moment the boarding party swarmed across. The pirates were hard experienced fighters, but

124

nothing in their repertoire was a match for the naked hatred and furious lust for revenge that motivated the newly freed slaves. For them an impossible dream had just been realised. The men who had beaten, tortured and starved them, worked them beyond the limits of endurance and laughed at their pleas for mercy, were now within reach of their swords and axes. The fighting was as short as it was bitter. The boarding party swept the corsairs before them like leaves in an autumn gale. Dead and dying pirates, brutally hacked and mutilated were hurled over the starboard side. The galley slaves were freed and armed. One – a long, lean desert nomad with the proud features of a chieftain – addressed me in perfect, but slightly accented, Darian.

'Greetings, Black Lion of the North. I am Angyred, Prince of Tra.'

I looked up into a pair of dark brown eyes that reminded me of someone else – the inn-keeper's wife in Kalaford – Ambala the dancing girl. She and Angyred were of the same race. His was a tall, proud, masculine strength; hers a lithe, sinuous, feminine beauty. The minds behind those eyes were similar too: lightning fast and highly intelligent. In every sense, these men and women of the Great Desert were a *noble* race.

'You are surprised that I speak Darian?' I realised that I had been staring at him.

'No. You remind me of a friend in Kalaford.' Quickly I told him about Ambala.

'You are observant, Black Lion. She is indeed of my house and lineage. I thank you for the service you rendered her. She is happy with her inn-keeper, and I give my blessing to all who give happiness to my tribe.' The dark brown eyes were looking right through me, searching about among my thoughts. There was no suspicion or idle curiosity in them. The Prince of Tra probed my mind as a doctor probes a wound – to find the extent of the damage and then heal it.

'You are deeply troubled, Black Lion,' he said softly.

'I am,' I admitted.

'You are torn with anxiety. The woman you love most is in danger.'

'She is the reason I'm here in Barak, destroying the corsairs who captured her.'

The deep, dark eyes had taken in and comprehended the scene.

'We must destroy or capture those three galleys,' he said softly. 'Give me this ship and I will attack them from the starboard side. Take your original vessel and row to port of them. They must not reach your raftsmen.' He looked at me once more, and what I read in those eyes would have led me to trust him with my kingdom, let alone a ship.

'We shall meet again soon, Black Lion, for I believe that I can help you to rescue your Amana.'

I scrambled back aboard my own galley and set the men rowing after the three vessels ahead. They were far to the south now, and moving in to intercept the central section of the Darian convoy. I doubted whether Angyred and I could reach them before they hit the nearest rafts.

To the north-west I could see Uxal's men who had already landed lashing rafts together to form a kind of pontoon. I could not understand his purpose at first, then I realised what he was planning. Thirty or forty rafts lashed together would form an unsinkable island. The fast flowing current would sweep it downstream – when he was ready – and bring the men aboard it into a position where they could attack the corsair galleys and pick up survivors from any capsized rafts. As I turned my attention again to the pirate ships in the south, the leading corsair rammed a Darian raft about 300 metres ahead. The raft reared up and broke, spilling soldiers. I saw corsairs on the deck of the galley firing arrows at the men in the water. Instead of trying to escape from the deadly armoured prow of the pirate galley, the other rafts in the area were now turning *towards* the corsairs. A soldier of Dar does not consider retreat – the greater his danger, the more savagely he attacks. The rafts, although slow and clumsy, were not as helpless as I had feared they might be. They were surrounding the galleys like vicious soldier ants swarming towards some larger animal which has strayed into their colony. Arrows were going in both directions now. It is not easy to fire accurately from the swaying deck of a crude log raft, but the bowmen of Dar are second to none, and the huge black shafts were already decimating the pirates on deck. We closed the gap separating us from the action.

I moved the tiller slightly to starboard and felt the galley responding. 'Row,' I shouted. 'Faster. Harder.' The ship strained forward. I swung the tiller through another ten degrees starboard and felt the jarring impact as our ram splintered the stern of the corsairs' vessel. I lurched forward, off balance for an instant, then sprinted the length of the deck and leapt over the broken stern planks. My first concern was to finish the pirate bowmen who were still firing at my men in the water.

There were loud cheers and blood-curdling Darian war cries from the nearest rafts as my soldiers realised what was happening. Several of the men in the water were swimming towards the galley now, swords drawn and glinting as they cut the foam. I hewed down the nearest archer and threw a loose rope over the side to a Darian swimmer. Using the dead pirate's bow I put a shaft through the chest of a second bowman and hurled a third into the water. There was another jarring crash as Angyred's galley struck the corsair vessel, and then the Prince of Tra joined me.

Back to back we fought the corsairs as their decks ran with blood. Then this fight too was over, and the slaves were free. I stood against the rail and surveyed the last vestiges of the battle. I had underestimated my raftsmen, or overestimated the corsair galleys. My mind had been creating grim pictures of drowning Darians ever since I had seen the tactical advantage the galleys had against my rafts. I had not allowed for the greatest of all Darian characteristics – the refusal to accept retreat as a serious alternative. If the raftsmen had attempted to get away from the galleys, then the reinforced prows would have played havoc with them. The Darian reaction had been to surround the corsairs and swarm aboard.

Uxal had also released his chain of joined rafts. Like a huge branch torn from a tree at the water's margin, the rafts floated south. Strong hands hauled swimmers from the water as the raft-chain passed. One galley had turned north to try to escape the encircling rafts. Angyred and I waited to the east. There was no escape past us, or past the newly freed slaves on our galleys. They were already baying like starving hounds for pirate blood. The escaping galley tried to tack northwards as we headed west, but the raft chain wrapped around it like an anaconda. A shower of heavy black Darian arrows cleared the deck, and a score of powerful infantrymen leapt on board in their wake. There was no resistance worthy of the name. The pirate ships were finished as a threat to my raftsmen. The army of Dar could cross the Abarak as it chose on the captured galleys, or go north and take the bridges.

Suddenly I was aware of Angyred of Tra close beside me. There was an urgent light in his deep brown eyes.

'You gave me back my life, and freedom from the hell of the rowing benches, Black Lion,' he said. 'I can never repay that in full, but I will do what I can. You must reach Ramos without delay – I do not know how I know; but I am certain that your Amana is there, and in danger.' His words reminded me of Nyrblos and the disc. I took it from the wallet at my belt and held it out for him to see. 'I too have a way of knowing without knowing how.'

I left him at the rail while I climbed the mast. Even as I ascended, the galleys we had captured were ferrying Darians over to reinforce our bridgehead on the quayside of Barak. They commanded the passage of the river; the Tiger held the stone guns above the harbour; Varon defended the landing places. The pattern was complete. The corsairs of Barak were finally subject to the King-Brothers of the north. I reached the mast-head and held the disc as high in the air as I could. The vibrations began slowly, as though Nyrblos was experimenting with wavelengths to locate me. Then they leapt up to an audible crescendo that sent my mind spinning; the disc resonated like a harp string. I felt a sudden biting, tearing pain across my back, as though a sea-hawk had dived with outstretched talons – yet there was no bird in the sky. The battle had frightened them away, though they would return later to their grim feast. The disc vibrated even more wildly, its pulses synchronised with a second slashing agony across my shoulders. Over the sound of the disc I heard a distinct gasp of pain. It was Amana's voice. I looked desperately at the empty sky. 'Where are you?' The disc moved even faster; it grew warm in my grip. And then the sky was not empty: I *saw* Amana – a pale, three-dimensional image of her with clouds and blue sky showing through, fainter than a rainbow. Her hands were chained above her head. Her long black hair had been lifted forward across her breasts to expose her back for the torturer's whip. I knew that she could see me in the instant that I saw her. Our eyes met across the sky. Her lips framed one word, 'Ramos'. Then with her next sob of pain the picture faded. The disc's vibrations died away, and I was alone at the mast-head.

As I reached the deck, Angyred laid a hand on my arm. 'Emotion and shock clouds your mind. Trust me, and do as I say.' The eyes of the Prince of Tra held only friendship and sorrow. My own mind was still a spinning vortex, a maelstrom of turbulent emotion. I could think of nothing coherently – Amana was helpless in the torture houses of Ramos, a living toy for the sickest perverts on Derl Wothor. I knew that her one hope lay in the fastest and most effective action of which I was capable, so I followed Angyred blindly until my head began to clear again.

As the shock waves receded I realised that we were crossing the Abarak. I was almost back to normal by the time we reached the quayside. Apart from a few desultory prisoners there were no corsairs to be seen. Varon and Uxal were directing operations along the harbour wall, and the Tiger had descended from the ballista platforms to meet me.

'Leave the army and this city in the hands of your King-Brother, and ride with me to the Oasis of Tra. From there my swiftest riders can escort us to Ramos. Ask the Tiger to lead the captured fleet of Barak around the Headland of Charl to attack Ramos from the sea. Let swift ships sail ahead to

9

Kalaport to fetch your own fleets from the north.'

'What says the Tiger?' I asked.

The grim old warrior looked at Angyred searchingly. 'The Lion has found a true friend in the Prince of Tra,' he said, 'and I'll look after our Darians.' The gigantic old hands settled on my shoulders. 'We'll find you the best horses in Barak; I'll meet you in Ramos, never fear. Keep safe, King-Brother of the North.'

We set out minutes later, with two spare horses carrying food and water. Our route to Tra lay north-east across the Great Desert. Within half-an-hour's ride of Barak the irrigation ditches bringing water from the river petered out, and the desert began to take over. Half an hour more and red-brown sand was flying up beneath our horses' hooves. With nothing to do but ride, I could not keep my mind off what might be happening to Amana . . .

Chapter Fourteen

The Oasis of Tra

The sands of the Great Desert moved like the tide. In centuries long past the desert had been a fertile plain dotted with walled cities half as old as time. As the sand had devoured the cultivated lands and eroded the green pastures the inhabitants of those cities had moved away, or fallen victims to the encroaching wilderness. As the streams and water holes had failed, city after city had died and decayed. Now the sands came and went with the wind, exposing a ruin here, covering one there. Parched stones jutted like long dead bones from the dust of a forgotten cemetery. Crumbling walls scarred the cheeks of sloping dunes. Defiant boulders still marked the lines of legendary floods.

We rode north-east as hard as the horses could go. Angyred's race were born in the saddle. He was one with the tall chestnut. He and the horse understood each other's purposes while they fought the sand together. I rode well enough, but I lacked the magic ingredient linking the Prince of Tra to whatever horse he rode. At his direction we changed the pack horses with our own mounts whenever his subtle saddle-craft told him the animals were tiring. Only someone with Angyred's skill could have coaxed the animals so far and so fast without exhausting them.

We rested only long enough to take food and drink and

feed and water the horses. The desert night was surprisingly cold after the heat of the day. The rocks and ruins cracked faintly as they cooled. The sands settled with a murmuring whisper in the gentle night breeze. It was as though the ruins were reminiscing about their builders, sighing over long departed glory.

At the top of a tall dune I took the precious disc from my wallet and held it up to the starlight. Pressed between my palms, it began vibrating slowly and steadily. Its pulses were like the rhythmic breath of a sleeper. Almost imperceptibly the vibrations changed, growing lighter and faster. Like a faint patch of zodiacal light I saw the outline of a sleeping girl: Amana, my Amana, projected against a screen of stars. The image grew stronger and more distinct. The vibrations increased and intensified. Her face turned towards me and she sat up. Our eyes met, and once more I knew that she was aware of me. Her face became radiant; her eyes matched the stars shining around her.

'I love you,' I whispered to the stars.

'I love you, too,' she answered.

'I am riding to Ramos as fast as the horses can gallop. You shall be free, soon, my darling, I swear it. I'll tear that damned city stone from stone until I find you.'

'Be swift, my Lord, my love, and may the White Gods aid you.'

'Do you know *where* you're imprisoned, the street, the house?'

'There's a tavern opposite called the Red Moon. That's all I saw.'

'It's enough . . . ' Her image shivered and began to fade.

'Hold on, Amana, hold on. I'm coming,' I shouted to the empty night. Only the stars looked down. Contact was broken. The disc lay motionless in my hand.

'Angyred?'

'Yes, Mark.' I found strength and comfort in his presence. He was a kindred spirit.

'Will we reach her in time? What are they doing to her?'

'My knowledge is different from Nyrblos' magic discs. I

feel things inside. I *sense* them. It's intuitive.'

'How soon before we can ride?' I needed to talk to him, yet I was mad with impatience to go on again.

'We must give the horses a few minutes more. Do you really want to know what they do to slave women in the torture brothels of the League?'

'I must know how long we've got.'

'Six or seven days, at the most. When the customers want new girls, the ones they're tired of are taken out and burnt. There's a concave cliff outside Ramos, about twenty times the height of a man. It makes a natural backdrop for their amphitheatre. They sell tickets for the burnings, and there's an elaborate ritual. Customers buy the right to burn various parts of the victims' bodies. It goes on all day sometimes. They don't light the main fires until the girls are almost dead. Then the whole area blazes. That's about an hour after sunset. One subtle refinement of the torture is to take a slave girl down there to watch the others burning, and to make sure she knows that she's next. They pay well for that . . .' he said bitterly.

I looked at Angyred in amazement.

'How can you know all this?'

The brown eyes gleamed in the starlight. 'Because that is what they always do to the women of my tribe. You have seen Ambala. You know she is beautiful. These madmen of the League cannot enjoy beauty – they can only destroy it.' He gripped my tunic fiercely, his proud face drew close to mine. 'Lord of the North, Black Lion of Dar, I did not deceive you. I swore to help you save Amana, and I will. But there is another hope in my heart. You have untold thousands at your command; I have only a few hundred. I want to see Ramos destroyed, their whole accursed League destroyed. My nomads cannot fight their million mercenaries but your Darians can. By the White Gods, Mark. They fear you in Ramos.'

I clasped his hands firmly in mine.

'Angyred, Prince-Brother of Tra, do you think I can spare even *one* life in the city where the Queen I love has been sold into slavery? From the moment that Nyrblos's disc showed me her pain, Ramos was doomed. If I die trying in this incarnation, I shall return to try again until I eventually succeed. For every drop of blood that runs from her body a river of blood shall wash the streets of Ramos.'

'The horses are ready, Mark,' he said purposefully. We mounted again and rode like the wind across the Great Desert towards the Oasis of Tra. Night turned to dawn and dawn to midday. Still we rode relentlessly, resting, and changing the horses whenever Angyred felt they needed it. The sun began to sink in the western sky behind us. Long shadows of the horses pointed towards our destination. From the top of the next dune we saw the palms and richly emblazoned tents of Tra. The horses seemed to know that the long ride was nearly over. I looked interrogatively at Angyred as they pounded the sand with invigorated hooves.

'They are coming home,' he answered. 'The Tiger found us the best horses in Barak, and the best horses in Barak are stolen from the tribes of the Great Desert. The corsairs raid the land as well as the sea. They enslave our horses as well as our people.'

We reached the oasis and Angyred leapt down. A ring of tall bowmen surrounded us, then recognised their Prince and cheered loudly, saluting him with their bows high in the air.

'Warriors and brothers,' he shouted. 'Honour my guest: first, because he is the Black Lion of Dar, King of the Northlands and Brother to the Tiger; second, because he saved our kinswoman Ambala from the devils of Argath, and third, because he freed me from a corsairs' galley.' Angyred's men cheered again and raised their bows in salutation. An old man came slowly forward, supported by two young warriors. His sparse hair was silvery, his eyes dimmed by age. He had a long white beard and his wrinkled face was as craggy as the ruined cities we had passed. The old eyes turned towards me and their vestigial sight studied me. The old hands, frail and wrinkled, reached out for mine. The veins looked fragile and prominent beneath the dry brown skin.

'Black Lion,' whispered the old man, 'I have dreamt a dream concerning you. I saw a city of apes and monkeys who

134

had captured a lioness. They built a fire before a great cliff and gathered there to watch her die.' He paused, breathing heavily. There was a silence so deep that not even the sand seemed to move. 'A great lion led a pack of desert wolves against the apes, but all were slain in the gateway of the city and the lioness was burned.' He paused again. 'But then the dream changed. An old grey wolf spoke to the lion before he reached the city. He went in secret, dressed in an apeskin. Wolves too were dressed in the skins of apes. Then I beheld the strangest sight of all: the great Lion flew from the clifftop and stood beside the lioness in the place of fire. In my tent I heard a voice which cried, "Zoria, Prophet of Tra, Priest of the Desert, four-score years and ten have you lived, yet nothing you have seen is greater than this dream. Rise up and speak to the winged lion." And so I came, obedient to the voice.' Like a man setting down a heavy burden, Zoria released my hands and sighed deeply, leaning on his two companions for support.

Most of the dream symbolism was obvious enough. The cliff tied in with Angyred's description of the amphitheatre where the girls were burnt. The desert wolves were the warriors of Tra, and if a few hundred of us assaulted the gates of Ramos the League's vast army of mercenaries would swamp us. Weighed against Amana's life, I counted my own as nothing, but I had no right to lead Angyred's men to annihilation. It was the second phase I did not grasp. From the Prince's description the cliff was over a hundred feet high. How could I fly down to the fire? How could I get Amana away once I'd reached her? I turned to the old man, Zoria.

'*How can I fly?*'

The old eyes focused on me with difficulty.

'You must remember a thing from long past and far distant; before you walked between the worlds you could fly.'

What did it mean? The old priest was now so exhausted that it was impossible to question him further, and, in any case, I felt certain that he had already told me all he could. Before Zotala, the Tiger and I had left our original world in the doomed space ship that had become Kalun, had we possessed the power of flight? Had the ancients been able to levitate? Or was there something in my life as Mark Sable on earth that was relevant? The only thing I could do was follow the first part of the dream, and hope that understanding would come. I turned to Angyred.

'Can we obtain League uniforms? What do they wear in Ramos? Is it the same as in Argath?'

He shook his head. 'No need, some desert princes trade with them openly. The tribes who serve Kelnos frequently spend their gold in the torture brothels of the League. Some nomads pay to see their own kinswomen burn.' The terrible bitterness had come back into his voice. 'I'll send for robes to cover that Darian war tunic and we'll find a way into Ramos.' He sighed wistfully. 'The prophet spoke truly – but I'd have loved to assault their gates.'

'That time shall come,' I promised, 'and when it does you shall ride with me . . . and a million soldiers of the North.'

Angyred was typical of the men of Tra. There was no shortage of volunteers, but, in accordance with old Zoria's dream, we decided to ride in small companies a few hours apart so that suspicion would not be aroused when we reached Ramos. Our first group, including a dozen of Angyred's best men, was on the point of leaving when two riders from the north reached Tra. We were waiting for them to dismount and greet the Prince when I recognised them: Parlo the fat inn-keeper of Kalaford and his exquisite wife, Ambala.

I have rarely seen such pleasure on two faces. Excitedly they began telling Angyred of our first meeting in their inn. 'And Parlo struck down one Argathian with a wine jar,' I heard Ambala saying proudly. The beautiful dancer doted on him. It was several seconds before Angyred was able to break through their torrent of greetings and explanation.

'My kinsfolk, you are always right welcome in my tents, but today I must leave you in the care of my wives and children. I ride with the Black Lion to Ramos, and it is possible that we shall not return in this life.'

'My Lord Angyred, we were come simply as guests to visit our people in Tra, but in the service of the Lion we ride with you to war,' said Ambala.

'Do you really wish to aid me?' I asked, a plan forming in my mind.

'We owe you our lives, Lord,' said Parlo.

'You have already paid that debt with a broken wine jar,' I reminded him.

'It is a debt of love, Lord,' said Ambala, 'and such are never repaid in full, nor forgotten.'

'My Queen Amana is in the hands of the torturers of Ramos,' I said softly. 'A woman who dares enter such a place could be worth a hundred warriors on this expedition.'

'I will fight on any part of the battlefield to which my Lord sends me,' she answered.

'Fresh horses,' ordered Angyred.

'Parlo,' I asked, 'how is the road from Kalaford, down through my Eastern Feudatory?'

'Since your return, Lord, the Argathians have withdrawn. The battle of Kalaford cost them dear, and they are reluctant to fight you again.'

'Then the road is clear to Kalaford?'

'Yes, Lord, clear and peaceful.'

A further plan was growing in my mind as he spoke.

'Angyred, give Parlo an escort to Kalaford.' I turned to the innkeeper. 'I shall guard Ambala with my life. If she does not return to you alive, neither shall I. Do you trust me?'

'Lord, you are the greatest warrior on Derl. None could keep her safer. What is my task?'

'Ride back to Kalaford and tell Eldon to bring every man he can to the gates of Ramos. Tell him to summon my rangers and miners, and the farmers from the Eastern Feudatory. Tell him also to send Bel of Kalaport to every fishing village on the east coast and to bring the biggest war fleet he can raise. He may already have heard from the Tiger by sea, but I think your horses will be faster than the galleys, and yours is the shorter route.'

'My Lord, you have rescued the Tiger?' Parlo was ecstatic. 'He is well?'

'He is very well, and sends his greetings to Eldon.' As we spurred away to the east, Parlo and his small escort rode north.

We galloped until the horses needed rest, then once more I climbed a dune higher than its neighbours and took out the silver disc. I could not bear to watch her suffering, yet I *had* to know that she still lived; I had to let her know that we were closer and riding as fast as the horses could stride. Nyrblos's technique must have improved again as he became still more accustomed to us. The image was clearer against the stars; Amana's voice was stronger, and the pain that I shared with her for those few minutes was sharper and deeper than the whipping. This time she was secured in a kind of chair while the torturers used pincers on her feet. Between screams and sobs she managed to communicate some vital information.

One of the brothel's regular patrons was an Argathian soldier, a junior officer with a large private income. His name was Haik, and he had actually been outside the prison in Kalaford when Amana had cut Melak to pieces. Haik had recognised her a few hours earlier, and was even now watching the torturers extracting her nails. When the show was over he intended returning to Argath to tell Melak's brother, Luthol, that there was a very interesting prisoner in Ramos.

This Luthol was an aristocrat, a powerful politician in Argath, and Haik was anxious to secure his favour. He was also one of the most feared men in the League – an arch-sadist and Grand Master of the House of Pain in Argath.

There was a wave of agony more intense than any that I had yet shared with her. She screamed desperately. Her eyes closed and the image faded. She was temporarily beyond their reach. Angyred stood beside me. He was crying un-ashamedly. 'When the last nail has been torn out, the girl's feet are plunged into salted water,' he said in a voice of terrible quietness.

'How much farther to Ramos?' I asked grimly.

'At least a day and a night, provided the horses hold out.'

I groaned thinking of what they would do to her in those twenty-four hours. I longed for eagles' wings to reach her in time, for flight . . . *Flight?* I knew the answer now, if only we could reach Ramos in time.

'Mark, your face has changed. What are you thinking?'

'Of your prophet, Zoria, and the rescue he saw in his dream. I understand now how it's to be done.'

'Tell me.'

'Where can we buy oiled silk and ropes?' I asked.

'From a tent-maker.'

'And strong, light wood, like canes?'

'Again from a tent-maker.'

'Can we buy them in Ramos without arousing curiosity?'

'Certainly.' Angyred was looking at me strangely.

'I trust you and your men to the ends of Derl, but I do not trust the wind or the desert sand. Wizards have strange eyes and ears, and Wizards are welcome in Ramos.'

'You are wise, Mark, and I can live with my curiosity until your secret is revealed.' His brow creased into a troubled frown.

'Is the Place of Fire best for the rescue?' As he spoke, Angyred put a hand on the nearest horse, to test its readiness.

'No, but Zoria thought so, and we shall know more if Ambala can reach Amana.'

'The horses can continue,' he announced.

We mounted again and streaked away once more across the sand. The hours came and went. It was a long, weary, desperate ride. I wondered whether Amana was still unconscious after what the torturers had done to her feet. I wondered whether Teryn's rangers had reached Barak before the Tiger left. I wondered whether Parlo would reach Eldon before I reached Ramos. Had Bel received the message yet? Ought I to trust the old priest's desert vision?

Before the sun set again we had passed Argath, and Kiphol, central city of the League, was in sight to the south of us. Ramos was less than twenty miles ahead. Where the land dipped to form gentle valleys we caught glimpses of the sea.

Three Towers Bay lay to the south, beyond Kiphol, and it was across that bay that the Golden Tiger would direct the captured corsair fleet towards Ramos. To the east, stretching far beyond the bay, lay the great eastern ocean; from there Bel of Kalaport would bring the fighting seamen of Valdar south to join the attack on Ramos.

'We must slow down, Mark,' warned Angyred, 'pleasure seekers do not gallop like warriors. We have come to sample the sophisticated delights of Ramos, to spend our gold in the pleasure houses and to sell a slave girl who no longer amuses us.' He called his men together. 'Let no one mention Tra. We are the servants of Kelnos from here onwards.'

At a leisurely trot we reached the walls of Ramos and headed slowly for the huge gates, seven metres high and studded with iron. They were closed. Torches burned on the walls above, and guards patrolled the parapet.

'Gate-keeper!' shouted Angyred.

'The city is closed, stranger, return at day-break.'

'We have gold for a gate-keeper who admits travellers eager to spend their money in the pleasure houses.' There was the sound of heavy bolts being withdrawn. Powerful mercenaries on either side of the gate-keeper scrutinised us closely. Angyred held out a bag of coins.

'State your business,' ordered the gate-keeper.

'To buy pleasure and to sell a slave girl who has ceased to entertain us.' Ambala looked convincingly subdued and frightened. She held her hands behind her back as though they were tied. The gate-keeper opened the moneybag and shared its contents with his detachment of mercenaries.

'Enter, and enjoy your visit.' He reached up and pinched Ambala's thigh as she rode past. 'Not bad. She should fetch a fair price. Why are you selling her?'

'She was disobedient,' said Angyred vaguely.

'She'll soon learn obedience here,' laughed the gate-keeper. Ambala shivered. We rode slowly into the city. An emaciated beggar squatted by the side of a darkened building. Angyred held out a copper coin.

'Do you know the Red Moon tavern?'

'Yes, master.'

'This is for you now.' He gave the coin to the beggar who clutched at it fiercely. 'Two more if you can lead us to the Red Moon.' The promise of more money rejuvenated the man; his stick-like legs moved with alacrity under his rags. He led us as fast as he could through a warren of narrow streets, then stopped and pointed. A red crescent moon hung prominently from a pole jutting above a tavern door. Angyred handed over two more coins. For the first time I felt a twinge of pity for a citizen of Ramos. Then, from the building opposite the tavern I heard a girl screaming, and my pity died. Her screaming subsided and there was tumultuous applause. We whispered quickly together. I was to enter first as a customer. Then Wylan, one of Angyred's men, would take in Ambala and sell her. Her job was to try to find Amana in the women's quarters and tell her we were nearby. Xa, another of Angyred's men would buy Ambala back later. I was to stand by to protect her in case things went wrong.

Over the door of the building a bas relief in marble had been let into the wall. It showed a group of slave girls being auctioned, whipped, branded and tortured. I stepped under the mural and approached the paybox.

'Welcome, sir, are you from Kelnos?'

'How did you guess?'

'You look like a nobleman from the Great Desert, and many of the Lord Kelnos's men come here.'

'I have heard of your entertainments,' I said meaningfully. The man in the paybox was scrawny and bird-like. He reminded me of a vulture. A wizened claw came out to take the silver coin.

'Straight through, sir, you'll find a few good seats left near the stage. There's an exciting programme tonight, and, of course, your choice of girls whenever you like.'

I tried to look nonchalant as I walked through an arched doorway into the central entertainment hall. Oil lamps and candles lit the scene, and flaming torches protruded from brackets around the room. Two men were dragging an unconscious girl off the central platform to the slave quarters at the rear. It wasn't Amana. After a moment's delay the same pair returned with a fresh victim. She was very young, and long-haired like Amana, but not so dark. Her skin was lighter, too. They chained her to a central pillar so that she faced in my direction, and brought a small charcoal brazier on to the platform. It was glowing brightly and two long-handled irons protruded from the hot charcoal.

'Tomorrow, you go to watch the burnings,' said one of the torturers. She trembled visibly.

'The day after – you shall burn,' said the other. The girl's head drooped; she began crying.

'Tonight you shall taste the fire,' said the first torturer. He withdrew a glowing iron and held it in front of her face. The audience applauded. The girl screamed. I didn't think I could watch any more without interrupting them. I was on the point of reaching for my sword when Wylan dragged Ambala in.

'Where's the buyer?' he asked loudly. The audience looked towards the new girl with interest. A hawk-featured man in the front row stood up slowly.

'I'm the owner. What have you got there?' He spoke softly and smoothly; the words dripped from his mouth like poisoned syrup. 'Put her on the stage.' Wylan handed Ambala over to the torturers. They put the branding iron back into the charcoal, and pulled her to the centre of the stage. 'I'll need to see what I'm buying.' Ambala began to struggle. I remembered her speed and strength in the tavern at Kalaford, and realised that she was only acting now. All the same it was convincing. The audience was cheering. They had an insatiable hunger for variety.

'Strip her,' ordered the owner languidly. Ambala broke free, suddenly, and then stood graceful and dignified in the centre of the stage alone. With the poise of a professional dancer she stepped out of her robe. She looked lithe, beautiful and desirable in the flickering light. The audience gasped its appreciation. She turned slowly, looking coolly at the avid, upturned faces. Then she retrieved her robe and slipped it on again. Incredibly, as if they had rehearsed the act with

142

her, the torturers stepped forward and seized her hands again. The audience applauded. The owner stepped towards Wylan.

'It seems that my customers would like her. How much?' With ritualised care they haggled over the price, while Ambala stood watching them impassively. At last it was agreed and the gold changed hands. The price was high, but not out of line. It would still be possible for Xa to buy her back, if all went according to plan.

The proprietor led Ambala towards the slave quarters, handed her over to one of his guards and went back to the platform.

'We shall whip her for you later this evening,' he promised. The audience cheered. 'Now back to the branding.' The girl chained to the post shuddered convulsively. The torturers withdrew both irons from the charcoal and held them out for her inspection. She shrank back from the glowing metal. An expectant hush settled over the audience. Xa strolled in and made his way past the platform towards the slave quarters at the rear of the hall. He made a long show of inspecting the girls in the cages. There was a terrible scream from the victim on stage as the glowing irons touched her. Angyred and two more of our party entered casually. I was fighting an impulse to leap on the stage, cut down the torturers and free the girl, but the impulse was winning. Only the importance of finding Amana first held me back. Of one thing I was certain, if it took a hundred incarnations I would destroy the League. No one must suffer as these girls were suffering.

Xa was whispering to Ambala. At last he came towards me. He had completed his deliberate tour of the slave cages. His face was white. He caught my arm.

'Lord, Ambala has found out what we came to learn. Luthol has taken Amana. She dies in the fire tomorrow.'

'Where is she?'

'The girls don't know.'

'Get Ambala out quickly and we'll go,' I ordered. Xa engaged the proprietor in urgent conversation. I sensed possible trouble and moved closer. Apparently the proprietor didn't want to part with Ambala until she'd been whipped. The customers might be disappointed. It would be bad for business. The girl on stage gave another terrible, choking scream and slumped forward unconscious. I looked at the burns on her lovely young body and felt sick and angry. My fist closed around the hilt of my sword and stayed there. Xa produced a second bag of coins and the proprietor's eyes widened appreciatively. The coins changed hands and I relaxed a little. Ambala was brought over and given to Xa.

I waited as our party made their way out carefully in ones and twos, then I looked back once more at the girl on the stage, hanging half-conscious in her chains. Tomorrow they would show her the fire. Next day they would burn her. She had nothing to look forward to except humiliation, agony and death. I knew then that I couldn't just walk out. She would haunt me forever if I did. I beckoned to the proprietor and indicated the girl.

'Is she for sale?'

He looked surprised. 'She's scheduled for the fire. The burning's all arranged.' He sounded like an undertaker who had been asked if the corpse was for sale. But I knew that money still ruled in Ramos.

'*How much?*' I persisted. No it was too difficult. There was not enough time to make alternative arrangements. It was all very irregular. Did I not understand the customary procedures? There were many other girls for sale. '*How much?*'

At last, reluctantly, he named a figure. Just in time I remembered to haggle. I kept thinking desperately of Amana and of how time was passing. I handed over the money. The torturers seemed surprised as they unchained the girl and gave her to me. She looked dazed and uncomprehending as they draped the torn robe over her shoulders.

'Don't be afraid,' I whispered softly. 'I shan't hurt you. You're safe now.' She shivered and began to cry quietly. I put my arm round her waist and led her out. Angyred smiled as we emerged, but his eyes were glistening.

'I think I understand why all northmen love the Black

Lion,' he said gently. 'You could not leave her to die, could you?' I shook my head.

'We need somewhere to use as a base,' I said.

'The tavern?' asked Xa, pointing to the Red Moon.

'It'll do.' We booked rooms and went inside. Wylan and Xa checked the stabling. The men of Tra took great care of their horses. Angyred would have slept in a flooded dungeon and thought nothing of it, but he would never have put his horse in a damp stable.

There were a few simple desert remedies in the nomads' packs, and Ambala was already smearing soothing balm over the slave girl's burns.

'We don't even know your name,' she said softly. 'Who are you?'

'Yolissa. My father's a fisherman at Sharin in Valdar. We were blown off course in a storm and captured by corsairs. I was sold to that . . . *that place* where you found me . . . My father was chained to an oar . . .'

She broke off, staring at me as though she were seeing a ghost. Amana had looked at me like that when I had first found her on the road south of Kalaford. Yolissa clung to Ambala, unable to speak. Her mind was still dazed by the pain and shock of her ordeal on stage. Her eyes opened very wide, and she pointed a trembling hand towards me. 'You're the Black Lion,' she gasped, 'the one who came to Amana in her visions. *I saw you. I heard you.*'

'You saw me? You were with Amana in the cell?'

She nodded. 'Yes, Lord.' Her eyes were bright. 'She *knew* you would come. Even when they were hurting her, she kept saying it, over and over again. When they left us alone she told me about you. She said you would tear this city stone from stone to find her.'

'I will.'

Ambala had spoken to all the prisoners but one – the girl on the stage, Yolissa. The deep pity I had felt, the undeniable urge to help, the absolute impossibility of leaving her there to die: now it made sense. Who or what was out there, helping and guiding me in ways I didn't understand? Nyrblos? Zotala? The White Gods of Kalun?

'Luthol came for her a few moments before I was taken to be branded.'

'Do you know where he's taken her?'

Chapter Fifteen

The Place of Fire

She shook her head sadly. 'The girls say he is the worst of all torturers, and he uses many different places. There are hundreds of pleasure houses in Ramos, Lord. They could be anywhere.'

I held up the disc, but there was no response. *Nyrblos was not answering.*

'Was there nothing else that you heard or saw that would give us a clue?' I held her hands tightly and looked at her intently. 'Tell me exactly what happened when Luthol came.'

Yolissa closed her eyes in deep concentration.

'He said that what she had suffered already was as nothing to what would happen at the Place of Fire tomorrow. He said that before sunset she would be begging for the flames to end her pain. He spoke of Melak, his brother, and the deep joy of vengeance. She said you would come with the Darian army and destroy Ramos. He laughed and said there were no enemies within a hundred miles, but tomorrow she would scream loudly enough to be heard in Dar.' Yolissa paused, biting her lips. 'Right at the end before his guards took her out he said "The Eyes of Night are waiting". Could that have meant anything?' She hesitated. 'One of the cruellest things about the torturers is the way they talk in riddles. The audience usually knows what they mean, but the prisoners don't. They say things like, "You look cold; we will make you warm;" then they brand you. They said to me, "Your nails are too long; we will tidy them".' She held up a slim little foot. Her toenails had been torn out by the roots.

'Then "The Eyes of Night" must *mean* something, however cryptic,' I said.

'A tavern, or a pleasure house,' mused Ambala.

'Possibly,' said Xa thoughtfully.

'A street, or a square,' suggested Wylan.

'What sees in the dark?' asked Angyred.

'An owl or a cat,' whispered Yolissa.

'The Temple of the Cats!' exclaimed Angyred. 'They perform a ceremony there called the Vigil of the Dead. I don't know much about it, but I think it's one of the dark rites of Kelnos the Sand Wizard, and he's an ally of the League – when it suits him.'

'What is this ritual?' I asked grimly.

'The condemned are taken to the labyrinth of the sacred cats and the priests of Kelnos use the random movements of the animals as oracles. They also decide the order in which the prisoners are to die.'

'It's not much to go on, but it's all we've got without Nyrblos,' I said, trying the disc again. *Nyrblos was still as silent as the grave.*

'We need information,' said Angyred. 'I don't know where the Temple is.'

'There are beggars enough in Ramos to lead us, Lord,' said Xa.

The first beggar we encountered was crippled, but the second ran ahead of us through another maze of dark streets and alleyways, some so narrow that we had to ride in single file. Ramos was an ancient city; it had been a port since men first sailed the oceans of Derl. Many generations had contributed to its confusing warren of crooked streets. It was a curious *twisted* city, inhabited by twisted people.

The Temple of Cats stood in the centre of a small, paved square, a little way apart from the other buildings. Angyred threw a coin to the beggar who scuttled away like a crab.

148

We rode carefully around the Temple, studying it. This part of Ramos was strangely silent and deserted. The torches and lighted windows were fewer, the darkness thicker and more sinister.

Angyred detailed one of his men to guard the horses, while we approached the door of the Temple on foot. It was a curiously carved door, but I could not make out the detail of the bas relief in the darkness. They were animal figures of some sort, probably cats, and as I traced the design with my fingers it seemed that they were interspersed with human figures. The door opened with a faint creak as I pushed it, and we moved quietly into the dark interior, feeling our way carefully. The floor sloped downwards, and we trod cautiously. Curtains of some thick, heavy material barred our way, but we pushed them aside and moved on again. A wall confronted us, and we groped for a door. There were two, but one was locked, or bolted, and I didn't want to risk alerting anyone in the Temple by breaking it down. If Amana was here, involved in some weird Kelnos ritual, I reasoned that our best chance of rescuing her lay in arriving unexpectedly. We moved quietly through the unlocked door. There was a dim, red light ahead, which flickered like flame as we drew nearer to its source. Stealthily, swords drawn, we crept closer to the light. At this distance I thought I could smell smoke and hear the faint crackle of a fire.

The corridor through which we were approaching curved slightly, and the light grew brighter. The fire when we first saw it, had a strange, unnatural quality. It seemed abnormally *flat*, like the two dimensional image of a fire rather than the real thing. A few paces more and I understood why. Our route was blocked by a thick glass panel. On the other side was a small fire on an iron stand. The flames, bright yellow and orange, danced across the glass. The transparent wall which barred our way was only one side of a small inner chamber. In the centre of this crystal box a naked girl was spreadeagled against the black skeleton of a long dead tree. All around and over the tree climbed small dark shapes – cats!

Their green and yellow eyes reflected the light of the fire, so that it looked as though the prisoner was surrounded by hundreds of moving, disembodied lights – *the Eyes of Night*. There was no discernible pattern to their movement. They paced the floor, circled the glass wall and climbed over the girl and the tree at random. The fire flared up, as some particularly dry piece of fuel reached the flames. There was a shower of incandescent sparks. Several of the cats hissed angrily towards the fire and moved farther away from it. In the increased light I could see the bound girl clearly: *it was Amana*.

I flung myself against the glass with all my strength, but it did not yield. I tried again, but it was harder than iron. To see her and be unable to reach her was more than I could bear.

'Amana!' I shouted desperately. Her head turned in my direction. I was not certain that she could see me through the glass. I guessed that from inside the darkness beyond it would reveal little except reflections. A ladder appeared above the tree and descended until it reached the floor of the glass-walled chamber. Three men climbed down. Two wore the leather tunics of guards, the third was dressed in a long ornate, expensive looking robe. I guessed that this third man was Luthol. His face was hideous in the fire-light.

As I continued to batter helplessly at the thick glass I heard him speaking.

'The Eyes of Night, servants of the Mighty Kelnos, have made their choice. We go now to the Place of Fire.' His claw-like hand traced a pattern down her arm. 'You shall burn slowly, as befits a murderess. You shall suffer as an enemy of the League.' He turned to his guards. 'To the Place of Fire.' Her eyes never ceased to look at the section of glass wall where I stood. I could not understand why Luthol and the guards had not even glanced in the same direction.

Was there some strange trick of the acoustics which prevented their hearing the impact of my shoulder on the glass wall? They had her off the tree and tied to the rungs of the ladder now. It rose clear of the central chamber and took her beyond my range of vision. A minute later it began to descend again – empty. I threw every ounce of my strength into one last effort. Luthol and the guards were ascending the ladder. Only the cats padded around the weird crystal chamber. I hit the glass with the force of a tornado. It swung open unexpectedly and I reeled across the floor, crashing into the base of the tree with a force that snapped off thick black branches. Recovering, I scrambled up it and grabbed for the foot of the ladder which was vanishing above me. I missed the wood but caught the ankle of the lower guard and plucked him violently from the rungs. The cats, already angered by my precipitous entrance, were arching their backs and spitting towards the fallen guard. I jerked him upright and pointed to the space above us where the ladder had been.

'It's the only way into the chamber,' he panted. I dropped him and strode back towards the panel through which I had entered. As though their feline sixth sense warned them to stay away from my fury, the cats clustered together at the far side of the chamber. There was a click, almost a metallic sound, as the panel swung shut again. I pulled at it ineffectually. Angyred pushed hard from the other side. It remained solidly in place. There was a wild laugh from somewhere above, and I heard Amana screaming in the distance.

I lifted the guard high into the air and shook him violently.

'How do we get out?' I snarled. His face was white with terror.

'There is only the ladder, and that has gone.' I flung him savagely against the wall and watched his lifeless body slither to the floor.

'Angyred, can you hear me?'

'Yes, and see you.'

'Go to the Place of Fire and do what you can to stop them. I'll join you as soon as I can break out.'

'I'd rather stay and help you.'

'Never mind me, go.'

The berserk battle fury that had destroyed Orthos was building up inside me again. I threw over the iron fire stand

151

and swung it round my head like a club. Once, twice, and then again, I smashed the solid iron into the glass wall. At the third stroke the glass cracked and the iron broke in two places. I dropped the useless remains and looked for a new weapon. The cats had gathered in the highest branches of the tree for safety. They leapt away as I moved towards them. I put both arms around the tree and shook it loose. Then I lifted. The ancient trunk came clear and I swung it into a horizontal position like a battering ram. I ran the full width of the chamber and drove the heavy end of the trunk hard against the cracked panel. More cracks radiated from the point of impact, but the glass held. Twice more I charged across the chamber, multiplying the cracks at each impact. On the fourth blow the panel exploded outwards with a crash like thunder. I was out in the corridor again, and racing for the door.

In the dim light outside the Temple I saw a figure moving stealthily towards me.

'Lord,' whispered an urgent voice, 'it is Yolissa. I begged Angyred to let me stay and guard a horse for you. I said I would be of least use to him in battle, and at last he agreed.'

'Good girl, you think like a warrior.' I leapt to the saddle, wondering why Luthol's guards had not already surrounded the Temple. He had had too much faith in his glass wall. 'Did you see any soldiers?' I asked.

'A small patrol challenged Angyred as he rode off, but our men cut them down,' she answered.

'We need a guide to the Place of Fire.'

'It is north of the city Lord, they told us that in the cells, and I think I see the first trace of sunrise in the east.' She pointed to a pale touch of light low on the horizon. I swung the horse north and she galloped beside me. Like all northerners she rode well, but without the special saddle magic that characterised Angyred's men.

'You're a fisherman's daughter. Did you learn your father's trade?'

'I can make sails and mend nets, Lord.'

'Good. I shall need your help, if all goes well.' Within a

152

matter of minutes we had found the inevitable beggar on a street corner. He was too old to run, so I scooped him up on to the horse in front of me.

'A gold piece if you direct me to the Place of Fire,' I promised. His body felt like a puppet, just sticks and rags, as I held him. He smelt indescribable, but I scarcely noticed as I concentrated on the directions he gave me.

We left the maze-like tangle of the old city and headed for the newer northern outskirts.

'There, ahead of us. Do you see the great cliff?' asked the old man. I lowered him gently and give him the promised gold piece. We spurred the horses towards the cliff. The sunrise was growing stronger. Its light was already useful in the east. We rode around the amphitheatre studying the gates and walls. Even at this hour, the entrances were heavily guarded and watch fires flickered from the gateways. On the staging in front of the concave cliff a number of iron frames were set into the rock. Shackles dangled ready to secure the victims. Braziers and irons stood waiting between the frames. In the centre were stakes and chains surrounded by brush-wood for the final act of this sadistic drama. I heard Yolissa's gasp of fear and horror as she looked at the apparatus of death, and remembered that she had already had one en-counter with a branding iron. There was no way of making a surprise attack through any entrance gate. The cliff was Amana's last chance.

We rode east, then turned north again. A bridle path ran up the grassy slope at the back of the cliff. There was no difficulty in reaching the top, but it was at least forty metres above the stage. Having double checked the access route to the cliff top I turned back towards the city.

'Where are we going, Lord?'

'To find a tent-maker, and an oil merchant.'

The business quarter of Ramos opened early and closed late. I bought fine, strong cloth, bamboo poles and viscous oil without difficulty. We rode back to the cliff top and found a secluded hollow surrounded by tough, scrubby bushes. Yolissa helped me to stretch the cloth between the framework of tightly lashed poles. When the structure was finished we oiled the cloth to make it as airtight as possible.

'Lord,' whispered Yolissa, 'is it a flying machine?' There was terrible fear in her eyes.

'Yes. On Earth it was called a hang-glider.'

'Lord, what if it fails?'

'I shall die, and Amana will die. It must not fail.'

'What else can I do to help, Lord?'

'Pray to the White Gods. Try to find Angyred and tell him what I'm doing. If I reach that stage I'll need as many of our men as possible to cut our way out again. Tell Angyred I'll try to make for the most easterly gate. If all our miracles happen together, my armies may reach Ramos in time. If not, we shall meet in our next incarnation.'

'I will find him for you, Lord,' she promised, and moved slowly away with the horses. I carried the improvised hang-glider to the cliff edge and peered over at the stage below. The audience had taken their places and the girls had been brought on to the stage and shackled into the frames. The braziers were glowing and the torturers were withdrawing irons, inspecting them and replacing them. Amana was second from the end, and I could see Luthol's blemished face as he said something to her.

The crowd was beginning to grow impatient. Luthol moved away from Amana and tore the robe from the girl at the end of the line. The crowd cheered. Luthol called out a number and a man in the front row came forward eagerly. Luthol indicated the iron he was to use and the place on the girl's thigh where he was to brand her. I took a firm grip on the glider and launched myself over the cliff edge. The flight was silent, except for the rush of air past my face. Every eye in the amphitheatre was on the glowing metal and the girl's thigh. Savouring every second, the man with the iron inched it forward. The girl screamed and shrank back as far as the chains would allow. Saliva was trickling from the corner of the man's mouth as he pressed the iron home. She jerked and writhed, screaming in convulsive agony . . . Then, a

154

split second before I landed, someone in the audience glanced up, saw me, shouted and pointed.

For such a rough improvisation, the hang-glider had performed magnificently. I made a perfect landing within two metres of Amana, released the bamboo and drew my sword. The hang-glider collapsed beside a brazier and the oiled cloth caught light. Some of the audience thought it was part of the show and began to applaud. I laughed, but there was no humour in the sound. It was the old, wild battle laughter, the madness of my long dead world. The fury swept over me as I saw Luthol. The laughter changed to the ancient and terrible words: '*Vashka, vashka, vashka! Niho zilan!*' They blended with the movement of the sword. The first blow took off Luthol's arm. He stared at it for an instant, in horror and disbelief. The next stroke took the top off his skull. The audience stopped applauding. There was a deathly silence. The burning wreckage of the hang-glider was giving off thick oily smoke, obscuring part of the stage. I reached Amana and tore the shackles away from the frame to free her. Down went the two nearest guards. Amana snatched up a dead man's sword and plunged it two handed into the back of the man who had branded the first girl in the line. He dropped the iron and pitched forward, blood oozing from his mouth. Still shouting my ancient war cry I struck down two more guards and hurled a glowing brazier into the audience.

'Break the chains, Lord, give them a chance,' called Amana. I ran down the line snapping shackles like paper garlands and hurling fire into the crowd. Another guard went down, stabbed to the heart.

'Eastern gate,' I shouted and leapt into the crowd. Someone crunched and pulped beneath me with a sickening scream as I landed. I looked round for Amana. She was a sword's length behind me and struggling over human debris. I cut down the man between us and she leapt lightly over the body. We cut our way ruthlessly towards the eastern gate.

The mercenaries had been totally confused so far, but now their officers were barking orders and re-asserting command. The gate was twenty metres ahead of us, but a large group

155

of soldiers was moving obliquely towards it.

'They mustn't take us alive,' I said.

'Kill me, if we can't reach the gate,' she answered. A sudden surge of activity in the entrance distracted the mercenaries. The gates were wide enough to admit a large crowd when necessary, and they were also wide enough for cavalry. Angyred, at the head of his tribesmen crashed through the eastern entrance like a steel tidal wave. The audience screamed and tried in panic to escape the flying hooves. The mercenaries threw up their shields to meet the new danger. I tore through the terrified crowd like a red hot knife through butter, cutting a path for Amana. Over my shoulder I saw that at least two other girls from the stage were following us through the carnage. The cavalry reached us, and close behind Angyred rode Yolissa leading an empty horse. I threw Amana up into the saddle.

'Get them away,' I shouted to the men of Tra. Angyred, Wylan and Xa formed a deadly rearguard as the cavalry ringed the girls and cut their way clear back to the gate. The two girls who had followed us from the stage staggered past and were swept up on to welcoming saddles by the nearest cavalrymen.

Angyred seized one huge gate and began to close it. Xa moved to help him. I hauled the other into place as Wylan hacked down the closest of the mercenaries. The heavy gates clanged shut, and we dropped the bar into its sockets. The amphitheatre had been designed to be secured from either side to facilitate crowd control. I leapt up behind Angyred and we spurred hard towards the rest of our cavalry.

'Head for the beach,' I ordered, as we galloped east. 'If the Gods are with us the Tiger's fleet may be on its way from Barak. If not, we'll ride north along the coast and try to reach my Eastern Feudatory before their mercenaries get organised. There's also a chance that Eldon and Bel are already on their way.'

Angyred rode up beside Amana and I changed horses as we headed for the beach. It felt good to have my arms around her again. There was still no sign of pursuit as we cantered over the firm sand. Her keen eyes scanned the sea to the south.

'Look, Lord,' she cried exultantly, and I followed her pointing finger. *The horizon was dotted with war galleys. The Tiger was on his way with the army of Dar . . .*

The Ballad of the Black Lion

Words by Patricia and Lionel Fanthorpe
Music by Justin Beynon

1. Though the wizard-spawn are lurking
   In the deadly burning sands,
   Yet the Darian clans are charging
   And their swords sing in their hands.
   There are noble desert tribesmen
   From the waterhole of Tra —
   Thund'ring hooves across the desert
   As they ride to fight for Dar.

Chorus: And when the Lion calls us
   We will ride from near and far,
   Across a thousand galaxies
   To fight the wars of Dar.
   From every friendly planet
   Orbiting a blazing star
   The Brotherhood will make its way
   To win the wars of Dar.

2. Sturdy fishermen of Kala
   Leave their nets upon the sand
   And wade through raging cataracts
   To join the Lion's band.
   Even White Priests of the Mountain —
   Peaceful for a thousand years —
   Lock away the sacred missals
   And reach grimly for their spears.

3. Watch the corsair fleet of Barak
   As it plunders and it kills,
   Till the pirates meet the miners
   From the rugged iron hills.
   Heartless mercenaries of Argath
   Selling honour with a sword,
   But the Lion of Derl Wothor
   Offers death as their reward.

4. See the hungry *jalnar* waiting
   In the shadow of its cave,
   And its massive jaws are gaping
   Like a newly opened grave,
   As it waits to do the bidding
   Of the wizard, its dark lord,
   Till it meets the axe of Teryn
   And young Iban's vengeful sword.

THE BALLAD OF THE BLACK LION

con moto

Though the wiz—ard spawn are lurking In the dead-ly burn-ing sands, Yet the Darian clans are charging And their swords sing in their hands. There are no—ble de-sert tribesmen From the wa-ter hole of Tra — Thundering hooves a-cross the desert As they ride to fight for Dar.

Chorus

And when the Li-on calls us We will ride from near and far, A-cross a thousand galaxies To fight the wars of Dar. From ev'ry friendly planet Orb it—ing a blazing star The bro-ther hood will make its way To win the wars of Dar